TALES OF THE CITY

A City of the Saved Collection

edited by Philip Purser-Hallard

Obverse Books
info@obversebooks.co.uk
www.obversebooks.co.uk
Cover Design by Cody Quijano-Schell
This edition published May 2013

All characters in this book are fictional. Any resemblance to persons, living or dead, is wholly co-incidental.

Printed and bound in Great Britain by Inky Little Fingers

CONTENTS

AKROATES

Philip Purser-Hallard

I had no real family when I was alive. My mother, who had conceived me in a moment of carnal frenzy with a passing herdsman, cast me out from her cave the moment I understood the rudiments of shepherdry.

She presented me with a pregnant ewe and directions to some pasture she had heard of far away along the coast. 'Now I have given you everything I ever will, Akroates,' she told me, and I was grateful.

That was the way my people were. Unsociable, solitary, belligerent. I truly believed until my dying day that everybody in the world was like that.

There were a lot of things I only learned after I died.

My people's mythology, for instance, was of the most rudimentary kind. So was our whole culture, given how rarely we spoke to one another with anything but anger or lust in our hearts. There was a tradition that our ancestors were the thunder and the lightning, and that they were created by the earth to be servants to the sky-god, but nobody really claimed to know.

(It was all rather vague. Indeed, to this day I have never discovered whether I lived in humanity's prehistory, or in some isolationist backwater of the posthuman cultures. All I can tell you is that our sun was yellow, our sky blue, our gravity roughly standard and that we had one moon. But all this would be true of any world humanity had reshaped in its image.)

Our notion of survival after death was confined to a nebulous foreboding that the sky-god might take advantage of it to punish us. Why he might feel the need to do so, or how we might go about dissuading him, fell outside the scope of our inquiries. Meanwhile, we lived out our dirty, uncomfortable lives: attending to our flocks' needs, ignoring our own, baking in the daytime sun, freezing on cave-floors at night, and all of us – although I cannot say I was aware of it at the time – reeking of sheep.

When I died – young, alone of course, of some lingering disease doubtless contracted from the unsanitary conditions pertaining in my cave – the only dwellings I had seen were holes in hills, the only artefacts crude assemblages of stone, wood or hide. I had met perhaps twenty other people in my life, most of them at no closer than yelling distance, and nearly all my conversations had revolved around the upkeep and ailments of sheep.

My feelings, then, on arising from death to find myself in a four-walled, second-storey bed-sitting room, with windows giving onto a view across the roofs of other pretty shingled townhouses like my own, down to a waterfront against which brightly-coloured houseboats bobbed like gulls, while across the bay beyond them glass-and-metal monoliths rose like blades to impale the clouds – and not a single sheep as far as my eye could see – are difficult to describe.

Or very easy, perhaps. Although at the time I lacked the words for this, as for almost everything not relating to oviculture, I fell in love at first sight with the City of the Saved.

It was complicated for all of us to adjust in the aftermath of Resurrection Day, I know that. Every one of us was in a place beyond our imagining, everyone was dealing with people and cultures and concepts and technologies which were beyond our sympathy or comprehension. As they emerged, the details of our new lives – the invulnerability of our new bodies, the shared language implanted in our heads, the literally astronomical size of our new home – confounded us again and again.

But still, it was trickier for some of us than others. However much I loved the City, the basics of urban living and of civilised interaction – using public transport, respecting other people's space, not defecating in a big pile of straw in the corner of my room – came hard to me.

In this, I was lucky in my new family.

It took some time for the idea of the *deme* to take root in the City. For some, whose deme consisted of themselves alone, returned to life in some solitary tent or bothy or autarkology, and similarly for those who were reborn in hive-like (but not Hive-minded) edifices containing tens of thousands of their new deme-kin, the concept was of little value.

Equally, those whose first families still held them in tight bonds of affection or tyranny – Sophia was one – would leave their deme in the City's earliest days and have only the most distant and polite contact with their resurrection kin.

Others, though, believe our demes were chosen for us. For us, the deme is a source of aid in trouble, of reassuring comfort in times of misery, a place of quarrels and shared memories, of loves and equally intense rivalries: a home to which, leave as we might, we cannot help but return. A family, in other words. For me, that group of seven human beings who were reborn in Number 67 Armistice Street, Motet Hill, Yerba Buena Bay, Calafia District, were the only semblance of a family that I had ever had.

Sophia left early, as I say: her father, Mr Maitland, placed an advert on the omniweb and one of the specialist finding services which sprung up in those early days brought them together. I rarely hear any news from her. In terms of the families which others – not, as I have said, I – remember from the first life, she is at best a far-removed cousin. Moody and Brianna are wanderers too, by nature – prodigals, you might say – but they keep in contact with me and with the others. Inigo and Lazarus found work elsewhere, though in very different spheres: they view me, I think, with the awkward and embarrassed protectiveness of older brothers. They are my kin, and it was only after death that I learned how gravely I had been yearning for such a thing.

Jane stayed with me for longest. She had little choice, of course, at first. Arranging for a wet-nurse to visit her – a woman who had died in childbirth and whose resurrection body was producing milk her long-lived son no longer needed – was, with the kind help of Brianna, the first use I ever made of money.

In traditional family terms, of course, Jane is – could only really be – my daughter. And, in the long tradition of daughters, she never writes.

I love her, though, as I love all of them. Even if they do all have that strange extra eye.

HAPPILY EVER AFTER IS A HIGH-RISK STRATEGY

Blair Bidmead

So there I was; dawn at the truck stop by the ziggurat at the mouth of the Mesopotamian Interstate. There was an inch of cold coffee left in my cup and my second cigarette of the day was down to a stub.

Trucks rolled by. No takers. It's like that sometimes. But that's OK. The City breeds patience.

I turned up my collar against the cold breeze and watched a cloud of pigeons scatter across the sky. A winged serpent chased the birds. Breakfast evaded the snake. This time.

I dropped the cigarette in the coffee cup, dropped the cup on the curb and shouldered my haversack. As the trucks weren't biting, I decided to try further up the road.

A chapter of VeloCentaurs roared past. I watched them disappear into the traffic before sticking out my thumb. I didn't want to risk a ride with one of those guys. Not after the last time.

The minutes passed by with the cars. An hour came and went. I was considering lighting up another cigarette when a ride finally pulled over. I'd never seen an automobile like it. Its mom must have been a Chevy Coupe and its daddy, a giant cockroach of some kind. It popped its passenger door like a beetle wing. I got in.

The driver said nothing as the car pulled away. He was a black guy, middle-aged, white hair and goatee. He was dressed entirely in white and his eyes were covered with mirrored glasses. I wished him a good morning and thanked him for stopping. No response.

I had no problem with this. If the guy didn't want to talk, that was his prerogative. I was the hitcher. He was the driver.

Except, when I looked more closely, I realized that he wasn't. Driving, that is.

The guy's hands were not on the wheel. He wasn't moving at all. I leaned over. The guy was asleep. And soaking wet.

'Sorry about that!' yelled a voice, making me jump. The voice seemed to come from all around me. 'That toll-computer can't stop, once she gets chatting!' chuckled the voice. 'Where y'heading, my friend?'

I searched around for someone to reply to.

The voice laughed again, 'Oops! Sorry, you're confused. Of course you are! Forgive me! I'm Cranzfraction. I am the vehicle in which you are currently travelling. You are..?'

'Terrence Moody,' I said.

'They call you "Terry"?' asked Cranzfraction.

'Nope. Just "Moody",' I replied.

'"Moody" it is!' chirped the car. 'Listen, Moody. Judging by where I picked you up, I'm assuming you're wanting to get the other side of the Rotherhithe Wormhole, yes?'

I agreed.

'That's what I reckoned,' continued the car. 'OK, strap in. We'll talk about how far you're going once we're out the other side. Hang on!'

The car accelerated. The traffic blurred. The Urukian District receded behind us. Approaching at terrific speed, the wormhole took us.

Colours. Euphoria. Nausea. Out.

It was raining when we emerged. We were tearing along a twelve-lane viaduct. It curved to the right, into a bank of grey clouds. Below us, skyscrapers and spires glittered in the rain.

'Are you OK with heights, Moody?' asked Cranzfraction. 'This is the Aphex District's Spiral Viaduct. It corkscrews down quite sharply in a few miles. I'll polarize the windows, if you like?'

'I am fine with heights,' I said. 'I used to be a pilot.'

'Really?' said the car. 'But now... you hitch?' Cranzfraction seemed to be calibrating its bullshit detector.

'Didn't work out so good,' I said. 'Which way are you headed, anyway?'

'I'm dropping this guy somewhere near the Uptime Gate,' replied the car. 'Is that any good for you?'

I had assumed that Cranzfraction was acquainted with the man in the driver's seat. Not so.

'Nah, he was hitching, the same as you,' the car explained. 'He flagged me down on the Achaean Suspension Bridge. He was soaking wet, gasping for breath. He managed to say was where he wanted to go, then passed out. Must a been exhausted, I guess.' The car changed gear. 'That being the case; I am afraid that you, Moody, are going to have to supply conversation enough for the pair of you. Understand?'

I forced a smile and explained that I wasn't much for talking.

Cranzfraction laughed. 'Well, I'm afraid I *am* one for talking, Moody. We have a long way to go and y'need two for a conversation! So, it looks like you're up, my friend!'

'What do you want to talk about?' I asked.

'Tell me about yourself,' said the car. 'You used to be a pilot, but it didn't work out?'

I nodded and confirmed.

'Nothing worked out. Period.'

Moody's Story

Flying lost its shine for me around December, 1941.

Back then, I was 2nd Lt. Terrence J Moody, United States Army, Far East Air Force.

I had a brief role in the South West Pacific campaign at the start of World War II. Very brief. Blinked, you would have missed me.

I was flying a P-40 Warhawk out of Clark Air Base, Luzon Island in the Philippines. I was a good pilot. We were expecting trouble. We were trained. We were ready.

I didn't even see the Jap that nailed me.

It was around 48 hours after Pearl Harbor. It was a routine patrol. We were tense, but like I said, we were ready. This time.

We were mistaken.

I remember noise. A fistful of gravel against an empty bean can. There was fire. Heat, but I can't recall pain. Smelled burning fat and fuel.

And that was what I did in the War.

Thousands of dollars worth of plane, all those hours training, equipping, feeding a soldier. All it takes is a pocketful of bullets, worth a pocketful of change and that's all she wrote. Never mind the Human Cost. Maybe we should look at the dollar cost for a change. Maybe that kind of crazy would make us stop.

So, I died and went to Heaven. It was no Heaven I ever learned about in Sunday School. The City of the Saved. I was out of my depth. Even within my deme. I was a farm boy from Iowa who joined the services. My life had been about working hard, going to church on Sunday and serving my country. That's all I knew. All there was.

I remember Faber, from my deme, asking me about the War. I didn't know anything. All the big stuff happened later. The atom bombs, the death-camps. I was already dead by then. Hell, I didn't even get the start date right. Could a sworn it was '41. Turns out it was '39.

He saw me as a walking piece of history. I felt like a dumb hick.

I died before I'd even got started. I don't just mean the War. It was worse than that. I'd got married the day before I flew out to the Pacific. I'd made my new wife a widow at 22.

Jeanie, that was her name. She was out there, somewhere in the City. I loved her as much as any man had loved a woman. I wanted to see her again, but I knew there was a risk. She was so young when I died. Chances were she'd remarried. Lived the life I had wanted, only with another man. Who would have blamed her? Not me.

I left it. I tried to keep busy. I worked various jobs. Gardner. Builder. Caretaker. Simple stuff. Stuff with my hands. On the ground. Jeanie was always in the back of my mind.

Then Faber showed me a book one day. I don't know why he had it. He was researching something. He's a serious academic type. It was a book about the Battle of The Philippines. I was in it. My name at least.

It said: *2nd Lt. Terrence J Moody, USAAF – MIA.*

MIA. Missing In Action. That was it. That was enough to tip the scales in my head. There was a chance. She'd loved me. If she thought there was a possibility that I might, one day have come home, maybe, just maybe she'd waited.

I was going to find her.

I could not have done it without my deme. All that omniweb searching. Talking to computers. That Flash Gordon stuff. I mean, I'm better at it now. I would have been lost without their help back then. I did the leg work.

It became a full-time job. It was an education. I saw the City up close at last, in all its terrifying glory. If I hadn't been searching for Jeanie, I am pretty sure I would have run away to hide.

And then I found her.

She was working as a receptionist. A place called the Warhol Factory. I walked in. There was Jeanie.

She was the most beautiful girl I had ever seen.

I mean, she looked different. She had gone native. Her clothes were... modern. But it was still Jeanie. She looked as old as the day I left her. She saw me. She ran to me. We kissed. It was a moment as perfect as any you see in the movies.

But, the credits don't roll in the City of the Saved.

Jeanie and I were inseparable. She told me how she had waited, how she had never given up hope. Even after the War. POWs were turning up years later. She knew, one day, I would come back. She knew.

Decades passed. Cancer took hold. Still she waited.

Eventually, the cancer killed her when she was 67 years old. She never remarried.

She had searched for me, in the City. I had kept such a low profile since I had arrived. Jeanie had drawn attention to herself.

We were happy. For a long time. Perhaps for not as long as I thought we were. But, at the start, we *were* happy. We laughed like children. I moved into her apartment. I got a job as a meat packer, close by. We made plans for the future.

One day I came home from work. She was crying. I asked her why. She said that she loved me. She had waited for me. All her life. Now I was here.

I told her I loved her too. I didn't understand why she was so sad.

She had loved a mysterious fighter pilot. A war hero. The perfect man. 'Til Death us do part.

Now she was living with a man who worked packing meat. A man who left the toilet seat up. An ordinary man. Forever.

Next to my own legend, I was found wanting.

We tried to salvage something. Start again. It was no good. When I eventually said that I was leaving, she didn't try to stop me.

If only they had recovered my damn body. She could have moved on. I wouldn't have come looking for her.

She would still have had the mystery.

I would never have lost her love.

I glanced out of the window. Cranzfraction swerved between gigantic, neon pyramids.

'A sad business, my friend,' said the car.

I shrugged.

'Strange,' said Cranzfraction, 'how things that seemed immutable, back in the Universe, can just wither away in the City.'

'It's ground me down, for sure,' I said.

'Down, but not out, Moody!' chirped the car. 'Listen, I am no stranger to heartbreak myself.'

'Do cars have hearts?' I asked.

'I'm AutoFolk, Moody!' Cranzfraction replied, 'I may be a car, but I'm as human as you!'

When I talk about it now, it all seems like it happened to someone else. I suppose, before the Grace of Civitata descended on me, I really was a different person.

Relax, Moody! I can feel you tensing up through the upholstery! This isn't going to be some born-again, religious hard-sell. 'The Grace of Civitata' is just a figure of speech. Although, it is a real thing too. Rewind.

I don't know how much you Dawn Humans know about my era. I come from Mechanique II. It was a major component in the Technosapien Interstellar Cooperative of the period. All my biological and technological inheritances originated there. It was an awe-inspiring place to grow up.

I worked in the Data Forge. Constructing algorithms for new emotions. I hadn't upgraded to AutoFolk then. I was humanoid. Same shape as you pretty much, give or take the odd port or appendage. I had a thriving love-support-network and I had MuVuThu.

MuVuThu was my Prime Partner. MuVuThu was my world. My inspiration. We met at the Data Forge. From the moment we first came into contact, our productivity at the forge spiked. We constructed emotions that were vast, yet delicate, intricate. Code of dizzying clarity.

Did you ever hear of the Summer Of Minus Ambivalence? No? We started that. Me and MuVuThu. Ask any Technosapien about that. They'll tell you. That wave affected everyone.

MuVuThu was the foundation of my Principal Self. Our love-support-networks entwined to become one immense maze of connections. Matrices of deep, nourishing affection. We shared so much of ourselves. We shared everything. Virtually.

Over time, our productivity at the forge levelled off. It never dropped, though. But, such an intense degree of output was unsustainable. MuVuThu and I were still fundamentally enmeshed. At least, that's what I thought at the time.

As time passed, I began to feel uneasy. MuVuThu seemed to be preoccupied by private sub-routines. Security protocols started to appear around MuVuThu's cessation periods. Priority communiqués went unreciprocated. It all came to a head when I discovered a stranger's data-shadow in our Mutual Relaxation Hub.

I confronted MuVuThu. The truth was devastating.

There was someone new on our love-support-network. Someone invisible to me. MuVuThu had begun a latent relationship with our Line Overseer, Niney Flanc9. My Prime Partner had been seeing the Boss behind my back. The full scale of the deception was revealed.

Now that the truth was out, MuVuThu wanted our partnership downgraded. Niney Flanc9 would be MuVuThu's new Prime Partner. I could stay on the love-support-network, but as a minor peripheral. This was too much. I couldn't process the information. My systems crashed. I rebooted in safe mode. So many corrupted files. How could have MuVuThu done this to me!? To us!?

MuVuThu could see that this proposed new set-up would be unworkable. Recriminations were already souring data streams throughout our Network. It would need to be a clean break. So, connections were severed, firewalls built and MuVuThu's beautiful wetware terminal was dispatched to Niney Flanc9.

It was over. I was a wreck. My Principal Self had been founded on MuVuThu. Sections of my personality were now missing entirely. The majority of our love-support-network had been torn away from me. What remained rallied the best it could. Affection was broadcast from all directions. Back-up personalities were forged to deal with my day-to-day practicalities, while my true self, heartbroken and corrupted, attempted to repair the damage caused by MuVuThu's departure.

I went into a decline. My new personality patches were tainted by the betrayal. My work at the Data Forge suffered. All I could think about was winning MuVuThu back.

I scoured our history files, looking for any clue as to where it had started to go wrong. Nothing seemed conclusive. I sifted through the remains of our mutual hopes/dreams cache. But the files were now so badly corrupted, it was useless. All that was left undamaged was a single image of a car.

The Car.

The X-treme Junction RoadMessiah 5000. Our dream machine. The ultimate piece of unattainable recreational hardware. We used to fantasize about owning one. Together. The Car was our future. It became clear what I had to do.

(Obviously, when I say 'It became clear', I mean from my perspective at the time. In hindsight, what's actually clear is that this is the point where I went hopelessly insane)

I briefly looked into buying a RoadMessiah, but the waiting list was endless and the cost astronomical. I couldn't generate that level of barter-code if I worked until the end of time. Instead, I decided I would *become* the Car.

Upgrading to AutoFolk is a medical procedure. So, the cost, while still great, isn't anything close to an expensive status symbol, like a RoadMessiah. It was still way more than I could legitimately afford. So, I decided to embezzle the Data Forge. Just like that. It didn't matter. I would become the car of MuVuThu's dreams! And if I failed to impress, I would run down Niney Flanc9!

You see how this was degenerating? How could it possibly end well? I remember thinking to myself that criminal sentences were much shorter for dangerous driving than for murder, that the upgrade would be a win-win situation whatever MuVuThu said! For Civitata's sake!

Madness.

I found a reputable counterfeit tech-surgeon, with glowing references from the satisfactorily upgraded. I ripped the barter-code from the Data Forge, leaving a trail of incriminating activity so obvious, I'm still surprised it took the Fraud-bots so long to find me. I dispatched my wetware terminal to the AutoFolk foundry and that was that. I was dismantled, reconfigured and reborn.

I was a car. The Car.

AutoFolk have a reputation for being arrogant. It's not entirely unwarranted and in my new form, I was no exception. I was going to win MuVuThu back. This wasn't even open for debate. I drove to a park where I knew MuVuThu's wetware terminal was often dispatched, to recharge the solar-cells and meditate. In my new form, I would no longer set off MuVuThu's GPS proximity alarm.

I don't know how long I circled that park, but eventually my persistence paid off. MuVuThu's wetware terminal was there, on a lawn, recharging in the sun. I blasted my horn with excitement. This did not go down well. Announcing myself as Cranzfraction, the former and future Prime Partner, impressed MuVuThu even less. It was downhill from there.

In hindsight, MuVuThu's reaction was entirely predictable. From a professional perspective, the emotional configuration of the rejection was, frankly, a work of art.

But, at the time, I couldn't understand or accept this rejection. I was the Car! I had turned myself into the status symbol of our dreams! MuVuThu must have gone insane! It was Niney Flanc9's corrupting influence!

I was so incensed; I didn't even register MuVuThu's parting words. My subconscious recorded them, of course. It was only when I listened back to the recording years later that I understood.

'The Car was always you, Cranz. It was never my dream.'

MuVuThu left me there, impotently revving my engine. Demented with self-delusion. It was just at that very moment that Fraud-bots began swarming through my Network. Game Over.

Except, so giddy was I with arrogance, I refused to give in. First, I did what no sane Technosapien would ever have done; I disconnected from my love-support-network completely. I suppose it would be the equivalent of you voluntarily blinding yourself. No, more like removing all your higher senses. Insane. I had bought some time while they scrambled hardware Fraud-bots to my physical location. I sped off toward the Data Forge. I swore that If I was going down, I was taking Niney Flanc9 with me.

But I was new to this AutoFolk lifestyle. I didn't possess the road skills that I have today. I took a corner at top speed. Crashed through a barrier on a flyover. Fell 200 storeys. Boom.

Dead.

And then on to the City. I don't have to tell you how disorientating that is, do I? Now, imagine that trauma of rebirth on top of my defective mindset. All I brought with me to the City, the only compulsion I possessed of any clarity, was hate. Niney Flanc9 was the focus of that hate.

Initially I based myself on the orbital M-Way surrounding the Turingesque District. I lashed together a basic Network, but it was incredibly superficial. I wasn't after human contact or support. I just needed information; Where was Niney Flanc9?

After a long, long time of following leads which went nowhere, I eventually found Niney Flanc9, living in the suburbs, scratching out a living, cultivating specialist digital root vegetables.

Finally, my target had been acquired. What then? No human in the City of the Saved can be hurt or killed. How could I deliver this hate that I had stored for so long? I decided that I would haunt Niney Flanc9. I would stalk, annoy, irritate and make this afterlife an eternity of suffering.

And that is how I spent the best part of 50 years. It could almost be funny if it wasn't so pathetic, so spiteful. Vandalism, hate mail, slander, noise pollution. I never let on why I was doing these things. It was just 'what I did'. Niney Flanc9 didn't know who I was or what had been done to deserve this treatment. By that time, neither did I.

Of course, several different authorities were called in to investigate; to catch the stalker. Every time that happened, I would just back off for a time, wait for the heat to die down, plan and begin again. This cycle continued until the day when I picked up a hitchhiker for the very first time.

I was just coming out of the carwash at the Junction 21 services – I had just completed a successful mission of wrecking Niney Flanc9's latest hidden allotment of digital veg. I remember wanting to clean the mud from my tyres. There was an old woman, sat on the kerb, silver-haired and silver-skinned. She was watching the traffic rejoin the M-Way.

It had never occurred to me to pick up a hitcher before. I don't know why I picked her up that day. Maybe I wanted to share my 'victory.' Maybe it was fate.

She was Proto-Technosapien, from a much earlier era than my own. She still had a recognizable gender and the differences between her biological and technological elements were far more distinct than during my time.

'What a beautiful car you are!' she said, as we cruised down the M-Way. I wasn't used to conversation and I had completely forgotten about compliments. I was confused. The woman went on: 'I bet you have seen some sights around the City, haven't you? Goodness, what freedom! Where have you been today?'

There was something about her enthusiasm. I thought about where I had been, earlier that day. I thought about churning up Niney Flanc9's secret garden with my wheels and, for the first time since my hate had ran out, all those years ago, I actually *felt* something.

I felt ashamed.

It was a feeling so profound, that my passenger, with whom I had no network connection, could sense my shame.

'My dear thing,' said the old woman. 'What could possibly make you feel so sad?'

So I told her.

I say 'told', but what actually happened is that we formed a basic support-network and downloaded each others experiences. It was tricky as our hardware wasn't compatible. She jacked in via my cigarette lighter in the end. The software took a while to synch and even then there were glitches. But given all that, this was my first true human contact since entering the City. It was both a humbling and a transcendent experience.

Her name was Litany Chromehurst. She was a traveller. She wasn't searching to find her place in the City as such. She just wanted to *see* it all. Experience it, first hand. To drink in all that human history had to offer.

She'd gotten about a bit, I can tell you. Dragon safari at the New Sanxingdui Arboretum, scaling the Immense Furniture of the Ispolini District, coffee and donuts with Saint Francis of Assisi. The list of events was so overwhelming I was rendered speechless.

In contrast, once Litany had assimilated my dubious collection of experiences, all she could say was: 'You're a bit lost, aren't you dear?'

Her gift for understatement is legendary.

And thanks to the straight-talking and endless patience of Ms Chromehurst, I began to make my first steps toward rejoining the Human Race. When I eventually dropped her off at her destination, something occurred to me. All the experiences she had shared originated from *within* the City. Unlike everything I had shared with her, there was nothing prior to her rebirth. As she stepped out of my passenger door, I asked her why there were no memory files from her previous life.

She paused for a moment, a brief look of incomprehension passed over her face, before she said, 'Oh, those old things. Got rid of them a long time ago. Didn't seem much point keeping them.'

I told you that the Grace of Civitata was real, didn't I? When it descended on me, she went by the name of Litany Chromehurst.

'Litany Chromehurst?' said a new voice. 'That name rings a bell...'

The man in the driver's seat was awake. The English accent came as a surprise.

'You're back with us then, buddy?' Cranzfraction chuckled.

'I am,' said the man, removing his glasses and rubbing his eyes. 'Just about. Where are we?'

'Midgard Underpass,' informed the car. 'There's a thousand-klick tailback. We could be here a while. You say you've met Litany?'

The man stretched. 'The name seems familiar... I can't place it. I meet a lot of people. Speaking of which...' He turned to me and extended his hand. 'Theo Possible, pleased to meet you.'

I shook his hand and introduced him to the car and myself.

'Good to know you both,' said Theo, smiling warmly. 'You would not believe the day I've had today...'

Theo's Story

I must apologize for my poor manners. In my defence, it has been a very trying day. It started off pleasantly enough. But later, through no fault of my own, things developed into a running-for-my-life type situation. Well, it was more 'pedalling' than 'running'. They were definitely going to kill me though.

Now, I know what you're thinking – 'Bloody tourist!' Mortality is a dead give away, isn't it? I am indeed a visitor to your miraculous city. Despite appearances, I am not human. Don't worry, I come in peace. In fact, I was invited to come here by an old human friend of mine. For his engagement party. That's what he told me, anyway.

The invitation came as quite a shock. In all the time I had known Steve – the human friend in question – he had never been very successful with women. Admittedly, a lot could have changed over the years since I had seen him. Although this didn't really explain how he was contacting me at all, what with him being dead and everything.

I have a most enduring image of the very last time I saw Steve. His nervous, apologetic smile as the Asymmetry Fiend lashed out and disintegrated him. Every cell in his body just wafting away.

Very sad, but an occupational hazard in our line of work at the time. I'm retired these days. Well, semi-retired if I'm honest. I've still been known to freelance on occasion.

Anyway, Steve died a long time ago, but here he was inviting me to his engagement party. What was that all about? Then I noticed the venue.

The City of the Saved. That exclusive little private members' club at the end of time. I had ended up in the City a few times before. I remember DJing at an after party for the coronation of Salvinder Heat-Death, the Hedonistrix of Eternal Intemperance. Sweet girl. Completely insatiable, mind.

Anyway, one mystery solved. Dead Steve was still dead and the afterlife seemed to have been working out for him pretty well. I RSVPed in the affirmative.

A few hours ago, I arrived at the Uptime Gate and waited, as arranged, at Lucrezia's Diner, just across the plaza there. There was no sign of Steve, so I had a coffee and a croissant while I waited for my cell-phone to synch up with the City's network. Eventually, Steve sent me a text message to say that something had come up and could I make my own way to the party. The Tube route seemed pretty straight forward, so I told him I'd see him there.

The train ride to the Achaean District was pleasant enough. I always say that you can judge a culture by the quality of its public transport. Strangely enough, I bumped into someone I knew. Small world, eh? I was lost in my headphones and felt a tap on my shoulder. It was a short, fat man who knew my name. Rather embarrassingly, I couldn't place him. He admitted he had changed quite a lot since we had last met. It turned out to be Obsèque Bleak of all people.

I'd completely forgotten about Obsèque Bleak up until that moment. He was, or rather had been, an arch-criminal from the 25th century that I'd locked horns with a few times, back in the day. My embarrassment was compounded further when Bleak reminded me that I was the one responsible for... dispatching him to the City in the first place. I mean, what are you supposed to say to that? A chance encounter with a man you'd not only forgotten, but the fact you'd killed him had also slipped your mind. OK, it had been self-defence and he had been a despicable bastard who had deserved it anyway, but I'm not a monster.

He took it amazingly well. He said that ending up in the City had been the best thing that had ever happened to him. So, in a way, I'd done him a favour. He'd moved on from crime and was now teaching yoga. He was really upbeat, positive. He gave me his card and said to drop in for a lesson anytime I was passing.

By human standards, I am exceptionally long lived – 'senior citizen' doesn't really begin to cover it – but even so; I never thought I'd live to see the day.

Anyway, I soon arrived in the Achaean District and, after weaving through the forest of colossal stone columns, I located the venue. A marble and crystal portico jutted out from a structure so large that it seemed to prevent even the concept of the uninvited from passing through. Given the security, this was clearly going to be some serious event. Dead Steve had landed on his feet.

There was a queue snaking up to the entrance where a six foot Amazonian in a PVC toga sat on a chrome bar stool, behind a red silk rope. She idly glanced at a tablet PC, avoiding the gaze of the meekly waiting herd with a pointed nonchalance. Behind her, like a row of up-ended limousines, stood five, surly-looking security-robots. I approached the Amazonian and gave my name. She smiled politely and checked her tablet. My name was not on her list.

Now, for any normal human, this oversight would have been the end of it; 'Your name's not down. You're not coming in.' Fortunately, my... People have certain disciplines not open to the... I was about to say 'Lesser Species' but it's not the politically correct term, is it? Should it be 'Regular Species'...? Anyway, unlike 'you lot', I am a highly skilled Charismatician. If I turn up to any social event, I am *supposed* to be there. On a very fundamental level, I am expected.

Put it this way: I can get them to squeeze me in at the Last Supper, if I ask politely. So, a smile to the Amazonian chick, a nod to the enormous robots, the red silk rope is lifted and I'm in.

Through the doors, I was amused to find myself at the beach. It turned out that the fortress-like building was, in actuality, just an impenetrable wall. Ahead of me, fine white sand stretched to a sparkling, azure sea. Throngs of bronzed bodies gyrated to tribal beats. The breeze carried brine, coconut oil, sinsemilla and barbeque smoke. I grabbed a margarita and mingled.

The party was so sprawling, it was hard to judge how many people were there. It must have been in the thousands. As I circulated, I noticed that as well as the dancing, eating and drinking, a variety of different tournaments were taking place. Along the beach, there was volleyball, Frisbee and jet-ski races. I spotted a wet T-shirt competition, a bodybuilding posedown and a stage where one man was using a stirrup-pump to empty a bucket of beer down another man's throat. All this was accompanied by whoops of encouragement from the crowd.

I found an empty sun lounger, near the shore and sat down to admire the view. To my left, the exquisite blue of the sea and the sky was interrupted by the gleaming lattice of a suspension bridge, so complex as to be verging on the impossible. It jutted to the horizon, carrying multiple lanes of speeding traffic, too distant to be heard.

A girl, somewhat worse for wear, sat down next to me. Clearly, she'd had a few too many of something or other. She turned to me, her eyes taking a few seconds to focus, and said, 'Theo Possible, you're here!'

I agreed. I was. Could this be Steve's fiancée? She looked like a trainee bag-lady. Apparently in her twenties, but with dark circles under her eyes and a grey complexion. Her hair was matted, her summer dress stained and torn. 'You've come to end it all,' mumbled the girl. 'The war stops, Theo. Be quick!' She pointed frantically toward the sea.

From the waves rose a woman as dazzling as a second sunrise. A bikinied goddess. She glided out of the water and across the sand toward us, deflecting admirers in a wake of indifference. She looked down at me, eclipsed the sun and said: 'Theo. So glad you could make it. I'm Heléně.' Heléně wrinkled her perfect nose at the wreck-of-a-girl sitting next to me and said, 'Sorry, Kassandra, I need to borrow Theo for a while.'

Drinks were suggested, so we fetched more margaritas, then wandered along the shore. 'Steve has told me so much about you, Theo,' muttered Heléně, conspiratorially. 'I feel as though I know you already.' I was forced to admit that Steve and I had lost touch, pretty much completely, since his tragic vaporization. How had someone like Heléně fallen for someone like Steve anyway?

She caught my drift and suppressed a smile. 'I've never met anyone quite like Steve before,' she admitted. I couldn't tell if this response was coy or just diplomatic.

We came to a small, wooden jetty. Helénē pointed to a swan-shaped pedalo and told me to hop in. Along the jetty, we had to step over a stoned-looking surfer, waxing his board. 'Yo, Hel,' said the surfer. 'Who's y'friend?'

Helénē untied the pedalo in a hurry and blurted introductions, 'Theo, Menelaus. Menelaus, Theo.' I exchanged nods with the surfer and clambered on board the swan. As we started to pedal out onto the open water, my perception developed an itch. I asked Helénē who it was that we had just spoken to. 'Menelaus?' she asked, all innocence. 'Oh, he's my husband.'

I took a moment or two for my thoughts to coalesce into something less irritable. When that failed, I just had to ask, 'You're Helénē... of Troy?'

The Most Beautiful Woman in the World threw me a sheepish smile and replied, 'For my sins.'

So, the engagement party I had been expecting turned out to be the Siege of Troy. Typical. Helénē explained that what had began as a bloody and grinding war of attrition, evolved into an endless beach party of banana-boat races and drinking bouts. Once in the City, the Greeks and the Trojans, now unable to kill or harm one another, were still compelled to compete. Helénē being the Grand Prize.

'It's got to be an improvement on a war, I suppose,' Helénē admitted. 'But, I'm just completely sick of being passed back and forth between Paris and Menelaus at the turn of every season. It's ridiculous. The Universe can end, but the stupidity of the Mediterranean male carries on regardless.' She began to pedal harder.

So, Helénē was a prisoner. She had the run of the place and was treated like a celebrity, but she could never leave the Spring Break of Troy. Her every move was watched. How could it not be? She was The Most Beautiful Woman in the World, after all.

The swan approached a marker buoy. Beyond it, the sea darkened. Deep water lay ahead. I then realized why Steve had invited me here. I was a Charismatician. I can walk past security like it isn't there. I can chat to the prom queen and no one will bat an eyelid. Steve knew this and saw it as a way for Helénē to leave the party – on my arm.

Of course, I was very flattered. The trouble was, applied charismatics can only get you so far. The combined forces of the Greek and Trojan armies were not about to let me sail away with history's greatest beauty, whichever way I styled it. The swan-shaped pedalo was a nice touch, admittedly. But even so.

I was about to voice these concerns when the swan was rocked by a large wave. I was thrown forward and I grasped at the swan's neck. A U-boat had broken the surface of the water, just the other side of the buoy. Behind me, I heard a splash. Helénē was in the water. At first, I thought she had fallen in. The pedalo was pitching violently. But no, she had dived in and was swimming toward the sub at a rate of knots. A hatch opened. Helénē hopped inside. The U-boat submerged and was gone.

There were shouts from nearby surfers. I glanced back toward the beach. Not everyone had seen what had just happened, but enough had noticed that everyone'd know soon. Already the surfers were paddling towards me. Things were getting awkward.

I pedalled.

I headed towards the bridge. I didn't look back and didn't even think. I just put everything into pedalling. I became one with the pedalo. I swam the last couple of meters to the base of the bridge and luckily found a service elevator. It was only once I was inside that I risked a backward glance. A thousand-man extreme-watersports armada was just meters away, with jet-skis closing in fast. The lift doors slid shut just as the first beer bottle hit.

On the bridge, I hitched a lift and the estimable Cranzfraction here very kindly picked me up. I was safe. It was then that exhaustion finally caught up with me and I passed out.

And this is where I came in.

Cranzfraction pulled into the rest-stop at the Uptime Gate plaza. A crystalline VeloCentaur was parked nearby. It waved as the car approached. Cranzfraction tooted its horn in reply.

'Who's that?' asked Theo.

'Just a racing buddy of mine,' replied the car. 'Here we are, Theo. Sorry the City's hospitality has been so lacking during your visit.'

'Not at all,' said Theo. 'Spending such an agreeable journey with two such fine people as yourselves has more than made up for the earlier unpleasantness. Please, let me buy you both a coffee or something.'

'You're very kind, Theo,' said Cranzfraction. 'I am afraid I must decline. My crystalline friend over there is demanding my attention. What about you, Moody? Going for a coffee or coming for a burn?'

I voted coffee.

Cranzfraction popped both doors. Theo and I clambered out.

'I just realized, Moody,' said the car. 'You never said where you were headed.'

'I didn't, did I?' I replied. 'Thanks again, Cranz. See you around.'

Theo nodded to the VeloCentaur as he passed. 'Great day for the race!' growled the Centaur.

'Which race?' asked Theo.

'The Human Race!' cackled the Centaur and with squealing tyres and blasting horns, Cranzfraction and the VeloCentaur chased each other across the rest stop and away into the endless traffic.

Lucrezia's Diner was busy.

Theo told me to choose anything I liked from the board. As we browsed, we heard a voice calling out Theo's name. We turned to a nearby booth and saw a thin, pasty looking guy with a bald head and a ponytail sitting opposite a stunningly attractive woman wearing an ill-fitting grey sweater.

'You've got a nerve,' Theo muttered.

The man gave an apologetic smile. 'You've every right to be upset, Theo...'

Theo cut him off. 'Upset? I was almost killed, Steve! You completely dropped me in it!'

'I know,' said Steve, holding up his hands in contrition. 'It wasn't the plan. I got nervous. I had to get Heléné out of there!'

'And I could get torn apart as a distraction, yes?' Theo snapped.

'I knew you would be alright,' said Steve. 'You always are.'

Steve's eyes cowed. Theo's stare flinched. A moment of deep silence passed. I glanced at Heléné. She met my gaze. I struggled to look away.

Eventually, Theo narrowed his glare, pointed a finger at Steve and pronounced, 'You're buying breakfast.'

'Of course!' Steve agreed, brightly. 'That's why I'm here! Anything you want! C'mon, come to the counter with me. Choose anything. For your friend too. Money no object...'

Steve led Theo away, towards the counter. Heléné smiled and invited me to sit down. I sat.

'I'm Heléné,' she said.

'How do you do, ma'am,' I replied. 'I'm Terrence Moody.' Heléné was just as beautiful as Theo had described. Her confidence was also as he had described. But there was something else, hidden in her eyes. An uncertainty.

'Have you known Theo long?' she asked.

'Just met him,' I replied. 'How long have you known Steve?'

'Oh, I've spoke to him on the omniweb for a while now,' she grinned. 'But I only met him today, in the flesh, so to speak.'

I reeled from the full intensity of her smile. She smelled like the ocean.

I said, 'So, is Steve your...?'

'He's a good friend,' she emphasized. 'I am... grateful for his kindness.'

I nodded and explained that I had heard about her earlier escape.

'So, what are your plans now?' I asked.

Helénē thought. 'Not sure,' she said. 'Let's see what happens.'

I smiled. Helénē returned the smile. With interest.

'What about you, Terrence Moody?' she asked. 'Where are you heading?'

I shrugged.

'Not sure, ma'am,' I said. 'Let's see what happens.'

THE SOCRATIC PROBLEM

Elizabeth Evershed

No doubt about it: Inigo Faber was having a dog of an afterlife, and as dog days went this was an uncommonly hairy one. Regrettably, the hair of his preferred dog, London Pride, was not available in the bar of the glitzy new college arrogated by the Director of Studies for this month's Board of Studies meeting. At his previous university such meetings had usually been capped at four hours and their tedium offset by a pint of real ale and a round-up of campus gossip at the pub afterwards. Here they could run on for as long as the participants' interest held, one of many half-arsed decisions on the part of the Administration which convinced Faber that none of the original architects of this so-called University of the Seven Ages had actually considered what would happen after they had cherry-picked 500 philosophers from several millennia of history and left them to 'get on with' the business of educating city-born undergraduates. In his experience, most philosophers did not 'get on' with anything, least of all each other, and he was no exception to the rule.

Faber would gladly have bunked this meeting if he could, but it would have been impolitic to miss out on any departmental business this year. When he had first taken up the University's offer of a semi-permanent lectureship a couple of years after Resurrection, the tenure review he had agreed to every 70 years had seemed a lifetime away – as indeed it had been then. But although his great reckoning had been a long time coming, it was only a matter of months off now. Faber knew his journal hits were negligible, which left him worryingly dependent on the goodwill of the peer-assessment panel if he wanted to retain his lectureship.

Thanks to the unremitting teetotalism of Shaw College's catering, Faber arrived at the Board alert and sober. He couldn't remember what the seating protocol was, and perversely chose the one seat vacant in the inner forum, forcing an entire row of logicians to their feet in an irate Mexican wave. The Director of

Studies, a 25th-century specialist in aesthetics, glanced up at him as he entered and pretended not to notice him. This was a bad sign, and to settle the swarm of panicked thoughts that followed it, Faber focused his attention on the other Board members. Besides the usual non-sequitur of logicians, the alter-metaphysicians were out in force, along with the whole crazy caucus of political philosophers. Only one solipsist had made it, and Faber's own discipline, ethics, was represented only by himself and a handful of meta-ethical relativists.

'Bored of studies, Inigo?'

That insouciant voice belonged to Jerry Spire, one of his former research students from the Bentham-Saatchi Institute in London. Faber hadn't noticed him come in and now he was sitting right behind him.

'I was just thinking how we never see you at the research seminars any more,' Jerry said.

'I've been busy.' It was best to keep it short with Jerry – short and light.

'Crafting your next magnum opus, no doubt.'

Faber forced a deprecating smile.

'Your lectureship's up for renewal next term, isn't it?' Jerry continued, although Faber was quite certain he was fully aware of the fact. 'Have you thought about... you know... your chances?'

'Just trusting in the process, Jerry.'

'Well,' said Jerry serenely, 'I'm sure virtue will out.'

Before Jerry, Faber had generally divided his research students into three types: the dull, but worthy; the genuine high flyers; and the brilliant but unstable, of whom he was secretly quite fond. Jerry might have fitted all of these types or none. That is to say, he was a consummate actor. So consummate, in fact, that Faber had never suspected him capable of the kinds of cut-throat opportunism he had demonstrated later in his career. Prior to his own death in AD 2089, relations between them had been cordial and Jerry a professed admirer of Faber's landmark study: *New Ethics of Love and War*. After he had been a few years in the City, however, Faber had been surprised to find the book returning a negative verdict when googling for his profile in the general catalogues. While all the sources agreed that *New Ethics*' influence on 21st-century ethics had been profound, by 2120 it had only merited a brief, disparaging wiki-note. Faber would not have minded so much if this crude hatchet job had been performed by some muddling hack, but its author had been listed as one Professor J Spire. Of course it would have been natural for his legacy to have telescoped over the years, but thanks to Jerry and his ilk it had virtually been hung, drawn and quartered.

When Jerry had turned up again at the University of the Seven Ages, like some ubiquitous scrap of flotsam, Faber had half-expected him to apologise for his behaviour or at least ape a little social awkwardness when they bumped into each other. Instead, he found himself treated with breezy condescension, even veiled amusement, by the younger man. To Faber, Jerry remained nauseatingly bright, superficially friendly, and dull as a weekend in Kempes District because of his constant hankering after promotion.

To avoid more conversation, Faber made an elaborate show of calling up the meeting agenda on his iBid. He had deliberately not looked at the document earlier on the grounds that he had better things to do with his time, but for once his tardiness had cost him more than he'd planned. Item number one concerned the nomination of candidates for the University's Visiting Lectureship scheme through which some distinguished philosopher from outside the University would be invited to join the department as a guest lecturer. The appointment was for three months to start as soon as possible and faculty were supposed to have come to the meeting with suggestions for candidates to approach.

It didn't take Faber long to see how this situation could be turned to his advantage. If he could somehow make himself indispensable to the process of finding a new lecturer, it might give him a stronger case for having his own lectureship renewed. The last holder of the post, Immanuel Kant, had been secured by the good offices of Professor Fichte, and his appointment had been regarded as a great coup for the University until his lectures were found to be as impenetrable in the Civil tongue as his treatises had been in German. It said something about the atmosphere of the department these days that it was only the Neanderthal lecturer, Baz Spear-man, who had had the courage to admit this to everyone else. They all knew Baz had been appointed to keep the Minorities Board happy, but he had a habit of cutting through the crap. Just as some ideas appeared to be over Baz's squat head, other, more ignoble, ones were patently beneath it: the notion that you might pretend to have more knowledge than you did, for example. In that respect, Baz could be as shrewd as Socrates.At the thought of Socrates, Faber experienced an involuntary shiver. What had begun as an idle comparison now seemed an inspiration from Civitata herself. Why had no-one nominated Socrates for a lectureship? Faber had hobnobbed with so many great minds over the years that he seldom felt the temptation to idolise them, but surely here was one luminary whose light could not dim on closer acquaintance. Socrates, that enigmatic seeker after the good, who was still known to half the citizenry as the father of philosophy... It would be better to encounter Socrates in person than almost anyone else.

But he was getting ahead of himself. The more he thought about it, the more he was certain someone in the Administration must have considered Socrates as a candidate before. He made some surreptitious queries on his iBid and discovered that the University had indeed made overtures to the philosopher to join them as a permanent professor when it was first founded. At that time the U of SA had been one of several independent Liberal Arts Colleges attempting to offer its students some synthesis of human wisdom across the millennia, and employing multi-generational, multi-disciplinal, and multi-cultural lecturers to achieve this. While the old Greek had been enthusiastic about the project, he had preferred to remain where he was. For him, he said, the search for wisdom must begin at home. Until he had found it among his fellow Athenians he would scarcely be equipped to recognise it anywhere else.

That had been Socrates' answer 70 years ago, but as far as Faber could tell he had never been offered the option of teaching in the department for just a few months. Given the time lapse and his original interest in the University, there was every chance he might accept the offer of a Visiting Lectureship now. He was certainly famous enough for the appointment to be acceptable to the Administration, and possessed an interest in more than one field of philosophy which ought to ensure him a broad spectrum of support within the faculty as a whole. Better still, his appointment would be one in the eye for Jerry Spire and the meta-ethical relativists. Faber would enjoy watching Socrates unpick Jerry and his arguments – preferably with a very fine toothcomb.

Tuning in once more to the buzz of talk around him, he was dismayed to find the meeting had already started.

'...and we're very keen to have a good communicator this time,' the Director was saying. 'Someone who can really connect with the students. Which is why I'm sure you'll all be interested to hear about Professor Spire's, well, *inspiring* suggestion at the Waste Disposal Committee yesterday. Would you say a little more about that for us, Jerry?'

Jerry took the floor with unctuous eagerness.

'While it would be a break with protocol for us to nominate another candidate from the second millennium, I think we could make an exception for the man so many of us think of as the *father* of philosophy...'

Faber flinched. The bastard must have been looking over his shoulder! But what did he mean by the second millennium? Socrates was definitely pre-medieval.

'I'm speaking, of course, of Rene Descartes.'

Faber buzzed in with a point of order. 'I always considered Socrates to be the father of philosophy,' he said.

'Ah, yes. Socrates...' Jerry raised an indulgent eyebrow. 'But you must admit Descartes to be the father of *modern* philosophy, Inigo.'

At this a few of the transhumans present began sniggering. Faber understood: the idea of any 17th-century thinker being ‘modern’ must seem ridiculous to the bright young sophs of the 30th millennium. In theory, all of the University’s staff were supposed to dialogue with each other as open-mindedly as possible, but in practice those academics harking from more recent periods of human history tended to look down on the researches of the older ones.

The Director called for silence.

‘Are you proposing Socrates as a candidate, Professor Faber?’

Faber nodded. ‘Surely we could all learn something from the *first* father of philosophy.’

The Director ignored the rather predictable point of order from Professor Heraclitus.

‘So you’re suggesting we appoint a man with no formal qualifications, whose reputation rests entirely on the works of another?’ Jerry quick-fired. ‘Personally, I’d have thought Plato was more suitable. At least he was the first *academic*.’

‘Shall we put it to the vote?’ said the Director.

When Faber finally stumbled out of the meeting nine hours later he was beyond the consolations of beer or bed. In the end, the support for both candidates had been split fifty-fifty until the Director had thrown her lot in for Descartes. How could some hidebound scholar of Aesthetics be given the deciding vote when everyone knew Plato had banned poets from his republic? And as for Professor J for Judas Spire, Machiavel-elect, apparently all he had to do was clap his hands and the entire faculty fell at his feet like dominos...

At the thought of the Machiavel – a popular figure of intrigue in the civic imagination – Faber experienced a second shiver of brilliance. Clearly the gods of the City were smiling on him today, reminding him of a similar incident several years ago. On that occasion the political philosophers had all been clamouring for Machiavelli, and even after the Director cast the deciding vote for Spinoza, they had refused to give up, enlisting the University’s charismatic Chancellor, Pico della Mirandola, in their cause. Pico was only too happy to put in a good word for a fellow Florentine, and his intervention would have been decisive if Machiavelli hadn't ditched the department at the last minute, in flagrant breach of contract, to take up a more remunerative offer at a rival school. Although the Chancellor was regarded as a liability by the Administration for his habit of interfering in University policy, there was no denying he was an effective poster boy for the University in the City, where his progressive syncretism was much admired. Faber had a lot of time for Pico, who, like most Renaissance humanists, was obsessed with Plato. This was the fact on which he was now pinning his hopes.

It was late when Faber reached his apartment, but he was pretty sure the Chancellor would still be up. He tried camming for him via the intercom and the steely eye of the buzz-cam directed him to a villa in Fell Dragon Park. Faber panned around the villa's spacious library and finally located Pico in a game of chess with a former Soviet Grandmaster. Faber projected a pint-sized hologram of himself beside the marble-topped chess table and waited for the Chancellor to notice him.

'Inigo!' cried Pico, more in welcome than surprise. 'Did you know the number of possible chess games is greater than the number of atoms in the known universe?'

Faber feigned astonishment.

'Georgy and I are endeavouring to map every single one.'

'That should take you a while, Mr Chancellor.'

'Ah, eternity's too short for everything I want to do!' said Pico, with a charming smile. 'But what's happening at the University these days? I get such dull reports from the Administration, I'm dependent on fellows like you for information.'

This was Faber's cue, but only when Pico had been fully warmed to the topic of life in the department did he make mention of the new appointment, and what a shame it was that Socrates had lost out.

'Who's the other soph?' said Pico, frowning.

'Some Frenchman from the 17th century,' said Faber casually.

'Civ's Bones! Now if it was an *Italian*, I might be more sympathetic. Dear gods, although I've never met this Socrates, I really do have to hold myself back from *worshipping* him sometimes! You know I keep trying to get Plato to do a lecture series for us? But it's been ages since I last heard from him.'

'Stupid trotsky,' growled Georgy. 'Set up his own district with a bunch of crazies who wanted their own Republic.'

'But how marvellous!' exclaimed Pico. 'Why hasn't there been anything about this in the news?'

The Soviet shrugged. 'What do you think happens to KaneNet reporters in a state run on the principle of strict adherence to accurate representations of reality?'

'I've just seen the time, Mr Chancellor,' said Faber diplomatically. 'Apologies for interrupting your game.'

Faber had no idea how successful his own gambit had been until Jerry Spire appeared outside his office the next afternoon with a face like Schopenhauer.

'I suppose you've heard,' he said. 'About the Visiting Lecturer. It's all been *terribly* embarrassing for the department.'

Faber brightened. 'You mean Descartes refused?'

'No, Monsieur Descartes' reply was very favourable. It only remained for us to send the official invitation to Upper Gaul when we heard from the Dean that there had been other arrangements. It seems our illustrious Chancellor has found us another candidate for the post, and with a colossus like Monsieur Descartes in the bag! Totally against protocol.'

'So who let Descartes out of the bag then?'

'Well, that's the curious thing,' said Jerry, staring at him very hard. 'In fact, I came here to salute you for a prophet, Inigo. It seems the man Pico hit on was Socrates.'

'But how extraordinary.'

'Now don't be so coy!' Jerry was actually wagging his finger at him now. 'The Director of Studies was most upset to think you'd gone over her head, not to mention the fact that Monsieur Descartes will probably never come to us after this insult.'

'I think there must have been some misunderstanding,' said Faber smoothly. 'I had better clear this up at once, Jerry, so if you don't mind...'

Evidently Professor Spire wasn't used to having colleagues retract their doors on him. Faber amused himself awhile watching Jerry fuming in the corridor. By the time he had unearthed his iBid, behind the bin, as usual (one of these days his collateral cleaner really would throw it away), he was in an obscenely good mood.

It was true: there were several messages waiting for him in relation to the new appointment. The first rather breathless communiqué from Pico he could not make head or tail of, but the one from the Director of Studies was clear enough: Professor Sokrates (she insisted on transliterating it the Greek way) would be arriving at the station the next morning, and a delegation from the University would be there to greet him, including the Director and Faber himself as well as the Dean of Humanities and a representative from the Administration. Faber gave a whoop of celebration, before deciding that he really wanted to celebrate the news with someone else. He considered camming his colleagues in the Bergson building to see who else was around, but on reflection he couldn't really imagine taking any of them out to dinner. In the end, he took the Tube out to the gastrozone by himself and spent the evening in Farquhar's Bar swapping Resurrection stories with a desperately chatty Medean ambassador with two heads. At least, he remembered the ambassador as having had two heads the next morning, but honesty forced him to admit that at that point he could well have been seeing double.

Socrates' welcome party was scheduled for midday so Faber had time to sleep in before ambling to the station. He had expected the philosopher would be travelling in on one of the high-speed shuttles from whichever Hellenic district he hailed from, but when he joined the others on the platform the Director informed him that their new lecturer had already arrived on an internal service after staying the night at one of Pico's palatine residences.

'So where is he now?' said Faber.

'How should I know?' said the Director (Jerry was right: she still hadn't forgiven him). 'He could be any one of those characters milling around the concourse. Seeing as this whole appointment's been sprung on us at the last minute, I never thought to google for his hologram.'

The Dean coughed. 'I have seen a picture, but...' He hesitated. 'I'm not sure it was *very accurate*.'

'I've got a banner,' said the Administration Officer.

The others watched while he unfurled a sign with the flashing legend:

WELCOME PROFESSOR SOCRATES!!!

'Dear gods, they haven't even spelled it right,' said the Director, with a shudder.

The banner had already begun to attract the attention of the arrivals on the platform, including a simian-looking figure who started waddling towards them very fast. Like most Neanderthals, he had bare feet and a distinctly rounded belly. His grotesque face and bulging eyes reminded Faber of an image in a book his grandmother had given him of a troll squatting under a bridge.

The Director glanced at the Administration Officer. 'He's probably attracted to the lights. So many of our primitive Citizens are illiterate.' Ignoring the Dean's frantic motions, she signed to the Neanderthal impatiently in Gestural Civil. — You big-thought man, or what? |

There was a moment's tension while the Neanderthal deciphered her gestures. Then he broke into a grin so wide Faber was almost afraid he might decapitate himself.

'My dear Citizens, I realise I may appear to you as 'a traveller from an antique land', but did you really think I would be some uncultured cave-dweller?'

They all saw the thick lips moving in time with the suave voice: a voice so utterly at home with itself it was impossible to think of its owner as Neanderthal.

The entire committee cringed at the Director's embarrassing mistake until the Dean, who was still bleary-eyed from a long night's boning up on Plato, saw an opportunity to say something clever.

'No, indeed!' he said hurriedly. 'No, *indeed*, Professor Socrates. We believe you to be one who has come up out of the cave, out of the darkness of ignorance into the one true light.'

'Eh?' said Socrates, fixing him with one of his swivelling eyes.

The Dean explained the Platonic allusion.

'Oh, *Plato*,' said Socrates, at length. 'You've read his books then, have you? Or novels, as I like to call them.' He grinned. 'Needless to say, I nearly had an aneurism when read all that! The poor dear boy did give me the most flaming character. Of course I was touched to find he was so cut-up after my death, but the trouble his books have caused me in the City! I can't even go to the agora now without some Citizen or other asking if I could speak at some conference for them, or model electric swimwear, or advise them on the best way to saddle a pack-horse. And then there are the religious types, asking me to arbitrate between this god and that, and all the unemployed poets wanting to know whether truth and beauty are one and the same or not... You know what I think?' He cocked his head towards them suddenly like a bird stabbing along the ground for a wisp of straw.

'What?' echoed the Dean, half mesmerised already by the relentless flow of talk.

'I think if they really wanted to know the answer, they'd learn to do a little thinking for themselves. Of course if I can help the process along in any way I'd be delighted, but unfortunately very few Citizens *want* my kind of help.'

'Well, I'm sure you'll find our students ready and eager to take advantage of all the help you can provide, Professor Socrates,' said the Director. (Faber could tell by her tone that she was still a little flustered). 'Personally, I'd be very interested to know in what respect you think Plato misrepresented your views. Perhaps you'd like to make that the subject of your inaugural lecture?'

'My dear woman,' said Socrates, holding up a hairy hand. 'Let us get one thing clear: when your excellent Chancellor invited me to spend a few months at your University, I only accepted the offer on the understanding that I would *not* be required to teach.'

The Director swallowed. 'But that's what the University is paying you for, Professor.'

'Oh no,' said Socrates gravely. 'I feel quite sure it would be wrong for me to accept money for lecturing on subjects I'm not qualified to instruct anyone in. No, as far as I'm concerned, I'm here to *learn*. Indeed, I'm quite thrilled at the prospect of studying at your venerable institution. But I'm afraid I may prove a very dull student for the lecturers. My dear wife always tells me I have the attention span of a gnat, and I think it's no secret that I have trouble following long arguments.'

Was the man caricaturing himself? Faber couldn't be sure. The old Greek seemed in earnest when he was talking, but he kept smiling at unexpected points in the conversation, making it difficult to gauge the levels of seriousness in what he said.

'I'm afraid there's been some misunderstanding, Professor Socrates,' said the Administration Officer. 'You'll have to provide four hours of teaching a week if you're going to fulfil your contract with us.'

'Perhaps,' said the Dean, with a tentative glance at the Director. 'Perhaps you might consider your role here as that of a visiting *researcher*, Professor Socrates? And if it's amenable to you, we would be delighted if you could share the fruits of those researches with us from time to time, perhaps for a few hours every week?'

'Certainly.'

Relieved, the Administration Officer handed Socrates an attaché case with the University logo on it: a seven-armed variation on the Vitruvian Man. 'You'll find all the relevant documents pertaining to your appointment in there. There'll be an opportunity for you to take a tour of the campus this afternoon, and this evening we look forward to seeing you at a special cocktail reception held in your honour.'

'Well, you *have* been busy,' said Socrates with a perceptible flicker of amusement.

'And now I'm afraid I must be getting back to the office,' said the Administration Officer. 'I wonder if I might have a word in your ear on the way, Mr Dean?'

'Bloody admins,' muttered the Director, after the Administration Officer had sallied off, the Dean following him reluctantly like a puzzled dog. 'I guess we'll have to postpone the welcome bash at the department so PR can get a piece of him. Well, I've enjoyed meeting you, Professor Socrates, but I won't deprive Inigo here of the pleasure of showing you to your new digs. After all, *he* was the one who recommended you to us.'

Faber experienced a strange shyness on finding himself alone with the philosopher.

'Do you have any luggage?' he asked.

Socrates shook his head. 'I'm afraid I left home in rather a hurry.'

Faber buzzed for a cab-car. 'I'd be happy to lend you anything you need.'

'That's very kind of you, Inigo, very kind, although I'm quite used to travelling light as it happens. Still, I must confess it was a most distressing circumstance that brought me to the Central District. Not to put too fine a point on it, I was actually forced to leave the Athenian Enclave.'

Faber waited for further explanation, but the old Greek was busy rummaging through the contents of the attaché case. He discarded several folders and a complimentary iBid as items that held no interest for him, pausing instead to scrutinise a small electronic tag.

'Your gym pass,' Faber explained.

'Ah!' said Socrates. 'They have a gym here, do they?'

Faber nodded. 'A state of the art one.'

'Well, that sounds delightful. I wonder if you would be so good as to take me there now?'

Faber hid his disappointment. 'Of course – if you'd prefer. I'll re-program the car to take you to your apartment after your work-out, shall I?'

'No, no,' said Socrates brightly. 'I much prefer to walk. Thank you *so* much for all your help, dear Inigo.'

The cab-car was already nosing its way towards the entrance of the leisure building, so Faber had no reason to linger.

'If you don't mind my asking, Professor,' he said, a little awkwardly, 'I'm confused as to why you were forced to leave the Athenian Enclave. I thought all Citizens were free to settle in any district they liked. Did you make the decision to leave on a matter of principle?'

The cab-car had come to halt. Socrates swung his bulk out of the seat and planted his stocky legs on the pavement.

'That's a very reasonable assumption, Inigo, but in my case I really was forced to leave.' Socrates glanced at the building behind them and lowered his voice. 'The authorities seemed to think I was a bad influence on the young... Oh, don't worry,' he added, seeing Faber's face. 'Of course I'm going to contest it. But I do need a more congenial place to stay right now, and I think we can flatter ourselves I've found one.'

'Whose idea was it to host a cocktail reception at Shaw College?' demanded the Director of Studies. 'No, I don't want another Virgin Mary, thank you, and if I needed more pretzels I'd have buzzed for them!'

The collateral waiter she had just harangued tried to make himself inconspicuous by taking on the colour of the faux-Corinthian columns behind him.

'Bloody shame, if you ask me,' agreed Jerry Spire, positioning himself between the Director and the buffet where he could best ingratiate himself with passing dignitaries. 'I think we could all do with a stiff drink to get us through an evening with the Vice-Chancellor. Except for poor Inigo. *He* needs a drink just to get out of bed.'

'Hello, Jerry.'

'Hello, Inigo. We were just wondering what you've done with our new lecturer.'

'Isn't he here yet?'

Jerry speared an olive. 'It seems he never made it on that campus tour.'

Faber had decided to keep the news of Socrates' exile private, but even without that worry he was beginning to have doubts as to whether this appointment had been such a good idea. As far as the Administration were concerned, Professor Socrates was not taking his new role seriously enough – which really meant he was not taking the Administration seriously enough, and this would do him no favours with the powers that were. After Jerry's comment, Faber was in some trepidation as to whether Socrates would turn up for the reception, but he did arrive eventually, escorted by a couple of security guards.

Most of the guests hung back when the philosopher entered, repelled, as the Director had been, by his fantastically ugly form. But after the Dean set about introducing him to the VIPs there was a gradual sea-change in Socrates' favour. The new lecturer's cheerfulness was subtly contagious and took the edge off the tension everyone else felt in the presence of the VC. Faber contemplated introducing Tarquin Tabor as their resident narcissist, but settled for describing him as the University's Vice Chancellor when Socrates drifted over to his side of the room to ask who the loudmouth in the burnt orange suit was.

Tarquin was already mounting the podium to make his usual speech of welcome. All but the newest faculty knew what to expect from this. While ostensibly there to eulogise the Visiting Lecturer, Tarquin always found numerous ways of praising himself at any public gathering. His excellent taste, superior political instincts, and strict control of the University's finances were fairly constant themes, and he had even been known to quote passages from his school reports verbatim. Next to their Vice Chancellor, even the solipsists looked like altruists. The PR Team always had a job keeping him to twenty minutes.

Socrates listened with the others until the Vice Chancellor finally got around to proposing that they raise a glass of soda water to their distinguished lecturer, after which a PR aide suggested he might say a few words.

Socrates nodded pleasantly, and waved his glass at the speaker. 'I see what you're about, my man. I think you were hoping, by your very flattering speech, to provoke me into a little flattery of my own! But while I have your attention, I wonder if I might satisfy my curiosity on one matter? You see, in my experience, it's quite a rare thing for a wicked man to boast of his wickedness, but you make no secret of your being the *Vice* Chancellor of this University. So unless by that soubriquet you mean to draw attention to the superlative virtues of dear Pico, I suppose we must assume you to be an *exceptional* man.'

'Why, thank you, Professor Socrates,' Tarquin murmured, with a beatific smile. At first he had been back-footed by their guest's startling speech, but now he was happily shoehorning it into a compliment.

'That is, either you must be exceptionally honest or exceptionally depraved.'

They could all see Tarquin blushing through his foundation. 'I'd prefer to think I'm honest,' he said, with dignity. 'And now...'

'Well, in that case,' interposed Socrates, fixing his interlocutor with his sharp gaze until he was wriggling like a beetle on a pin. 'Perhaps you'll tell us *which* vice it is you're chancellor of?'

At this point Faber, who had been growing more and more hot under the collar, decided to breach protocol by explaining to the philosopher, as audibly as he could, that his interpretation of 'vice' was a complete misnomer. The old Greek merely took advantage of the confusion to cruise the buffet. An aide segued the awkward break with music while the Vice Chancellor conferred with PR, and after that there were no more speeches.

Faber was so certain that his career was over he was not paying much attention to the talk around him. It was with some astonishment, then, that he found himself the object of approving smiles and surreptitious congratulations from colleague after colleague. It seemed the new lecturer had been a hit with the faculty, who were uncharacteristically united in their contempt for the VC, which meant Faber himself had just been promoted to persona grata for having inadvertently orchestrated the evening's showdown. Jerry was hard put to contain his envy, and even the Director admitted it had been a triumph for the department. Faber was ecstatic: against all the odds, the gamble with Socrates had paid off, and there was every chance it would pay dividends in future.

The next morning, for the first time in ages, Faber showed up at his office early. He ordered a coffee and began working through his messages, deleting a month's worth of increasingly passive-aggressive requests from the Administration asking him to confirm the date of his peer-assessment panel. He had just finished sorting through the pile of rubbish on his desk when the buzz-cam announced a call from the Dean of Humanities.

'Oh, Faber.' The Dean's anxious projection settled itself into an empty chair. 'I just received a message from Administration, and I thought I ought to let someone in the department know: it seems your Professor Socrates has enrolled himself as a student on various courses.'

Faber chuckled. 'Well, that's a bit unorthodox, but I can't see why it should present any problems if the lecturers are happy with it.'

'That's just it. Naturally he's welcome to sample any lectures he likes, but I don't think he's quite grasped the idea of what a lecture *is* yet. There have been complaints from faculty members. I wouldn't go so far as to say he's actually been *heckling* them, but...'

'You mean he's been asking questions?' Faber could see where this was going.

The Dean hung his head. 'I suspect he merely wants to encourage rigorous debate by challenging some of the, erm, *assumptions*, of his colleagues.'

'Well, why not?' said Faber. 'The students might learn something from it, Mr Dean.'

'Oh, I quite agree with you – in theory – but it seems in practice Professor Socrates' actions have been viewed as undermining the lecturers' authority.'

'Alright, I'll talk to him about it,' said Faber resignedly. 'I don't suppose you have any idea where he'll be this afternoon, do you?'

The Dean's projection froze a moment while he consulted. 'The next lecture he's booked in for is Professor Heraclitus' "World of Change".'

Heraclitus' lecture had already begun when Faber slipped into the darkened auditorium. It was impossible to tell if Socrates was there or not; the rows of heads in front of him were barely visible in the semi-gloom. Faber decided to wait it out, hoping not to fall asleep in the meantime. As it turned out, there was little opportunity for that: Heraclitus was exploiting the properties of newly-discovered technology. Faber was shocked at first, and then highly diverted, when a burst of fire announced the Professor's entrance onto the speaker's platform. Next a three-way screen with surround-sound bombarded his audience with time-lapsed images of moving water. By the time the accompanying monologue had started Faber suspected that they were, in fact, being treated to a clip of the same river running on a continuous loop.

Earth to Water, Water to Air, Air to Fire...

'Excuse me, Professor Heraclitus...'

Heraclitus paused, mid-flow. 'Who's that?' he said, frowning into the dark.

'I've always been an avid reader of your work, but I do have a few questions about this "world of change" you keep harping on about. What kind of change are we talking about here? Do you mean that everything is always *moving* or that it is always *altering in substance*?'

'Both,' said Heraclitus impatiently.

'But when you say that everything is always changing, do you mean it's changing in both senses or one?'

'I mean both, of course. Now if you would just let me continue with my...'

'Because if everything was only changing in one way, and not the other, it would not be correct to say that *everything* was changing, would it?'

'That's right.'

'But then in that case our senses' perception of this change would be in flux too.'

'I'm afraid I can't see how any of this is relevant, Mr...'

'I only mention it because if everything is changing in the way you've described, none of our perceptions of it can be reliable. You see the very instance of observing change would also be an instance of *not* observing it, nor can we talk meaningfully of something's having one quality rather than another if these qualities are never fixed...'

The voice stopped. Heraclitus had begun heaving like a punctured halibut.

'I'm not trying to trip you up, Professor,' Socrates continued. 'I'm just trying to get the argument straight. Can you still say that the world is in a state of flux, if – as we have just demonstrated – our very apprehension of that state must always be dependent on *something's* being constant?'

Faber managed to nab Socrates on his way out of the lecture hall – no mean feat as the old Greek ran out of the room as soon as the talk had ended.

'Inigo!' he said, slapping Faber on the shoulder. 'What did you think of Heraclitus' performance?'

'I think "performance" was the operative word.'

Socrates laughed. 'If you'd like to walk to the gym with me, we could talk about it on the way.'

'Actually, I came to see you on an errand,' Faber admitted. 'You see the Dean thinks it would be better if you stopped asking questions in lectures.'

'Dear me, that is odd! And when it was practically the Dean's idea that I should! If I'm here as a researcher, I ought to be allowed to get on with my research, don't you think? How am I to accomplish that if I'm not allowed to ask questions?'

'Of course you should get on with your research, whatever that is...'

'Prospecting for wisdom, Inigo – prospecting for wisdom as other men pan for gold.'

'Well, I'm glad you mentioned panning, because that's what it looks like to *them*, Professor Socrates. I'm not saying you should stop asking questions altogether, but couldn't you do it somewhere less public? That's what the other students do; if there's something they don't understand they drop in on the lecturers during office hours to talk about it privately.'

'Well, I've tried that once or twice, but either they won't let me in or else they refuse to debate with me. Believe me, I don't wish to make a nuisance of myself, Inigo, but the only place I can get a straight word out of any of these so-called experts is their lectures, and not always then. Even Heraclitus was lucid in comparison to Professor Wittgenstein.'

'You talked with Wittgenstein?' Faber was impressed.

'We *had words*,' said Socrates ominously.

Faber sighed. 'Look, Socrates – if I can call you that – I'm only saying this for your own good. You see, there've been some complaints.'

'Well, I *may* have gone too far in needling Heraclitus, but I had always thought him to be the sort of man who would welcome a rational discussion of his theories.'

'I think you'll find most faculty prefer to discuss their theories *outside* the lecture hall,' said Faber firmly. 'Although,' he added, as an afterthought, 'you might make an exception in the case of Professor Spire.'

Faber had reason to hope Socrates had taken his advice when the next two days passed without incident. The next morning, however, the philosopher surfaced at one of Faber's own seminars accompanied by a gaggle of students who seemed to have adopted him as their mascot. To Faber's relief, he ventured no questions, but sat staring into the middle distance like a man possessed. Faber was just wondering whether he ought to be concerned about this behaviour, when the philosopher came to, kissed several of the young male students effusively, and departed, arm-in-arm, with Zebulin Torque.

'Does Professor Socrates often go about with Zebulin?' he asked the other students after the seminar.

'Is he a Professor? I just knew him as Socrates,' one of the girls shrugged. 'Yeah, he and Zeb are pretty tight.'

Faber held off from asking any more questions, but he had to admit this new development was worrying. Zebulin was a pretty boy – a bit of a hothead in some ways, but pleasant enough. Still, there were disadvantages to tangling with a Torque, and Faber couldn't help feeling uneasy at the idea of him and Socrates being intimate. If the Administration got to hear of it they would almost certainly disapprove, but he didn't fancy broaching such a delicate subject with the philosopher.

Faber returned to his office to find the Director of Studies waiting for him. It must be something important to bring her there in person; normally she would have cammed him with anything routine.

'Is this about my tenure review?' he hazarded.

The Director folded her arms. 'Have you any idea where Professor Socrates is?'

'I suppose you've tried his office?' said Faber, playing for time.

'As far as I can tell, he's never actually been in it. Or his new apartment, come to that. The rumour is he's been "couch-surfing" at the penthouse of one of our students, who also happens to be a prominent councillor's son.'

Faber decided to come clean. 'Look, I know Professor Socrates' behaviour has been attracting comment, but as far as he's concerned, he's only acting as normal. By his own standards and those of Ancient Athens, I mean. Yes, he's a little eccentric, but I can't see that he's doing anything *wrong*.'

'So you've finally joined the meta-ethical relativists, have you?' said the Director drily. 'You know what I'm talking about, Inigo. If it gets out that Socrates is having an affair with a student here, let alone *which* student, the good Citizens of Kane News will have a field day.'

'But we don't know that he *is* having an affair with him, Madame Director.'

'But you admit that his conduct towards this boy is inappropriate?'

'I don't see why it has to be. After all, he's very affectionate – and Greek. Anyway, I thought you wanted someone who could connect with the students?'

'This is no laughing matter, Inigo,' said the Director sternly. 'I'm going to have to caution him about this, and I've called an emergency Board Meeting this afternoon to address the other complaints. I suppose you heard about the debacle at Professor Wibble's epistemology seminar? Apparently, Socrates asked Wibble how he could justify drawing a salary if he was so sceptical of the communicability of knowledge.'

'There must be *some* faculty who appreciate his more inflammatory tactics. Professor Nietzsche, for example...'

'Nietzsche can't stand to be in the same room as him after Socrates told him – in front of his student – that he was barking.'

'What about Baz?'

'He appears to be the only one who's come off well from the encounter. I gather Socrates was quite taken with his "How to Start a Fire" lecture.'

'Has he made it to any of Jerry's lectures yet?' said Faber hopefully.

'Unfortunately Professor Spire's been off sick.'

Faber fought the urge to laugh.

'So if you see Professor Socrates, tell him to come to the Board meeting,' the Director concluded. 'And, no, I hadn't forgotten about your tenure review, but after the week I've had, you better pray the gods of the City like you more than I do.'

With such a morning under his belt, and the prospect of another Board meeting in the afternoon, Faber opted for a liquid lunch. He arrived at the meeting as late as he could, but even then there was no possibility of slipping in unnoticed.

The Director glared at him. 'If I may bring the meeting to an *official* start. Professor Abelard has received an explanation – I'm afraid we can't call it an apology – for absence, from our Visiting Lecturer.'

'Ah, yes,' said Abelard, raising his tonsured pate officiously. 'I ran into Professor Socrates at the gym this morning. When I told him about the Board Meeting, *he* said,' Abelard paused for emphasis, 'his, ahem, *daimon* had warned him not to come. I understand this *daimon* – a sort of familiar spirit, Madame Director – acts as a personal adviser to Professor Socrates, telling him which meetings he should or shouldn't attend...'

Faber bowed his head to the storm of derision that followed. He had entertained a faint hope that Socrates might be at the meeting to smooth things over, but he saw it would be impossible for the philosopher to redeem himself with the department now. It seemed odd that they had settled on this circumstance of the *daimon* as the final proof of their new lecturer's insanity, when in general the University's staff were among the most religiously-tolerant of the City's populace. Faber saw what it really meant, and might have been amused by in other circumstances: none of the them wanted to admit how perturbing Socrates could be as an interlocutor, or how, against their whole seven ages of research, one week with him had set all their carefully-spun philo-systems trembling like spiders' webs.

When at last he returned to the Bergson Building, it was almost nightclap. He had had some half-hearted idea of camming Pico for advice, but when he reached the office he found the light on and his collateral cleaner, Fillis, scanning for dust mites.

'...so you see, Socrates, when we first got together, I was really taken with his tail, but the longer you're with someone, the more you realise you've got to love them for the soul-stuff...'

'Hello, Socrates,' said Faber dully. 'I'm sorry about the cleaner.'

'As a matter of fact, it was Fillis I came to see.' Faber couldn't help noticing the philosopher was looking unusually well-groomed this evening. 'I'm glad I ran into you though, Inigo. I'm just off for a little symposium at Zeb's place. Care to join us?'

'Oh, what the hegel,' said Faber wearily. 'Civ knows I could do with a drink.'

In the years to come, Faber would remember that night at Zebulin's penthouse as one of the strangest of his second life. The entire suite was crammed wall to wall with students (most, like Zebulin, drawn from the City's elites), and all of them practically falling over each other to engage the philosopher in wine-fuelled conversation. They were insanely young, these city-borns – a mere nineteen or twenty – and in their clumsy, earnest surveys of the new world his words had opened to them, they reminded Inigo Faber of his own first love-affair with philosophy, back when philosophy had been a lifeline and not some minefield he was paid to cross. And that, of course, was how Socrates had always seen it; it was why his questions had more power than all their answers; it was why...

Faber woke, disorientated, to find himself stretched on the sofa in his office. The door had been left open, which was asking for trouble. Pretty soon it wandered in in the shape of Jerry Spire.

'I've been doing some research, Inigo.'

'Well, that's what you're here for isn't it, Jerry?' said Faber, regarding him unsteadily. If Jerry was here, then the party must be over – except for the one still thumping its way through his head.

Jerry watched him. 'It seems our new lecturer is not the only person in the City who shares his biodata. In the Athenian Enclave alone there are forty-two remakes of Plato's Socrates – and those are just the patented ones. How do we know our Socrates isn't one of them?'

Faber heaved himself up from the sofa. For once he was too tired to play their usual games of cat and mouse. 'Well, if he is a remake, he's done a good job of convincing us. And what does it matter really if he is one, at the end of the day? You know the alter-metaphysicians think we're all fakes – copies – of other selves, in other universes. And for all we know, they may even be right.'

Faber had never seen Jerry this angry before. Normally everything about him was dangerously controlled. 'Don't come the Platonist with me, Inigo! If you won't take this information to the Administration, then I will, and I'll tell them you did nothing about it!'

'Whatever, Jerry. I don't give a foucault.'

A few minutes after Jerry had left, Socrates appeared in the doorway with a tumbler full of water. Faber was touched to think he had gone to the effort of finding one in the building. Apparently no-one had told him there were quicker ways of getting a drink.

The philosopher observed him coolly, like a scientist. 'You know, you did rather overdo it last night, Inigo. You're still not a happy colour, even now.'

'Yes, well, Professor Spire's conversation will do that for you...' Faber took the cold glass and pressed it to his forehead. 'Look, Socrates. Jerry's turned the tables on me. I won't tell you what he said, but he's given me an ultimatum. Either I have to leave the University or betray a friend I've come to respect. But whatever happens, I think that friend will have to leave the University anyway. I just can't see another way out.'

'Well, we must take the most rational course,' said Socrates. 'You see I'm under no illusions as to who this "friend" is, my dear fellow. But I believe the gods may have decided the matter for us.' He pointed to a white disc with the University logo on it. 'Fillis has just given me this. Apparently they left it in my office.'

Faber slipped it into the buzz-cam.

A projection of the Administration Building appeared with a pre-recorded message:

The University regrets to inform Professor Socrates of the early termination of his lectureship, as per item 3A of his contract. We have serious concerns about the Professor's suitability as an instructor of young people. The Professor will please leave the University by nightclap or be forcibly removed. If he wishes to appeal...

Socrates' expression barely registered surprise. 'You'd think they could be more original.' He composed himself a moment, then reached for his coat. 'Now, Inigo, don't make a scene that is unworthy of you.'

'But I won't let them do it!' cried Faber. 'This is the last straw!'

'Well, Heraclitus was right about one thing,' said Socrates quietly. 'When he said a drunk was like a boy leading a man. I think you've let the boy lead long enough. What does the man say, Inigo?'

Faber turned to the window and looked out onto the quad which any minute now would be overrun with Kane News reporters. He watched the tiny dots of students and lecturers beetle-tracking back and forth under the invariably white sky.

'Let's go,' said Inigo Faber.

LOST SHIPS AND LOST LANDS

Juliet Kemp

The train rattled away and back out of Cerulean District, leaving Brianna alone on the open platform. Roughly-hung posters, advertising cheap yacht hire and balloon-ship cruises, flapped at the corners in the breeze of the train's departure. Scaffolding hung off the station in all directions, interspersed with planks banged roughly together to create lean-to houses. Apparently, even the locals who chose to live on the nearest to solid ground the District offered didn't care for too much solidity in the way of their open sky. And really, if the closest you could get to solid ground was to build out from a station whose anchorage in reality was itself a matter of significant scientific debate, perhaps it didn't matter much how robust your buildings looked.

The stairs down from the station shook as Brianna stepped down onto them, and she swore, grabbing for a non-existent railing. The majority of Cerulean Groundbound's inhabitants might be well-equipped to ignore the vast depth of sky below them; she, currently, was not.

'Three days for two!' a grubby-looking woman with stubby insect-like wings, leaning in the doorway of a tour agency, called after her. Brianna carried on down the steps, digging into her pocket for the sketch-map. The gaps between the pavement-boards discouraged hurrying, even as the general down-at-heel feeling encouraged it. Falling might not be fatal here – she looked down through the boards and hurriedly averted her eyes from the depths of sky below – but she didn't think she'd ever come to care for it. The locals swung irritably past her, often coming off the narrow pavement altogether for a few wingbeats, before settling back onto their feet, and Brianna eyed them enviously as they flew past her.

The map was far from comprehensive, despite the effort it had taken her to acquire. She'd been hearing the rumours for a while now, in traveller-bars and hangouts across the City. The suggestion that maybe physical form, here, wasn't as fixed as everyone had assumed. That if the City's protocols forbade you from making physical changes to yourself externally, it might not forbid making those changes internally. People spoke over a beer of someone somewhere who'd altered their imago – alterations which varied in detail and plausibility according to who you talked to. There were darker rumours, too; if you could *change*, then perhaps also you could *damage*. Not everyone in the City was happy that physical intimidation was impossible here; not everyone was prepared just to settle down and accept that. Brianna'd heard the rumours, from time to time, but never really believed in them – just traveller's tales. And then she'd met Clara, and decided that maybe, finally, it was time to settle down and grow up and become the adult that she'd never managed to become in the Universe.

It took six tortuous months of domestic semi-harmony before she'd thrown a change of clothes and her lucky frog into her battered shoulder bag, and fled to her deme-mate Lazarus' place. She'd left Clara a note. At least, she was pretty sure she had. Somewhere after the tenth or eleventh beer with Lazarus, he'd mentioned the rumour again. Someone he'd encountered in a scuzzy hostel somewhere who'd boasted about changing his imago. She'd left the next morning, before Lazarus was up. If she couldn't settle down and grow up, she might as well keep right on chasing herself around the City. She'd always wanted wings. Why the hell not get them? And if she couldn't, well, it was as good a reason as any to go to the next place. After three weeks she'd finally managed to persuade an address out of someone – not even Lazarus' source, in the end, who she'd never found – and she still wasn't sure that she had the right of it.

The map took her to a part of Cerulean Groundbound even more down-at-heel than the station, and when she found the address, it took a good two minutes of knocking before she got any reply at all. Eventually, a young boy, head cocked on one side in a way that went very well with his beak-like nose, leant out of an upper window.

'What d'you want?' he demanded.

'I'm looking for Dave,' Brianna said. 'A friend sent me.' She felt there ought to be some kind of password.

The boy eyed her up and down. 'Right,' he said after a moment, then disappeared again. After a moment, the door opened, and the boy beckoned her in.

'He's in the back,' he informed her, unfurled his wings, and disappeared up the hole between the floors which would have been a staircase anywhere else.

Dave was sitting on a back veranda which overlooked – nothing. Well; sky. Most of Cerulean was sky. Lovely, empty, deserted sky. Brianna sighed wistfully, and Dave turned round. He was smoking something that smelt moderately disgusting, and his own wings emerged from a stained white vest with a ragged hole cut in the back.

'So,' he said. 'You're here about the imago change, then?'

Brianna's eyebrows rose a little at the blunt reference. No one knew exactly how the City's practical laws were enforced, but most people had a healthy wariness on the matter. She wasn't sure whether Dave's insouciance made her more or less nervous.

Still. She nodded.

'Right. What d'you want, then?'

'Wings,' she said. 'I want to go out there.' She gestured at the empty spaces of Cerulean. 'I want wings.'

'There's not a whole lot out there,' Dave said dismissively.

'That,' Brianna said with feeling, 'is the point.'

'It's permanent, you know,' he warned her. 'Unless you come back and pay again, that is. You sure you don't just want a dinghy? I can send the kid out for one. Save a lot of hassle.'

Brianna shook her head. 'Wings,' she said again. 'I've got the money.'

Dave shrugged and threw his cigarette end out into the blue expanse. 'Right you are, then. Sit yourself down over there, and let's see the colour of that money before I get started.'

She'd expected to hesitate when it came to handing over the majority of her resources, and was faintly surprised not to feel anything beyond mild relief. She couldn't, she reflected, go back to

Clara now, even if she wanted to. Dave ruffled through the notes, nodded, and gestured for her to sit down, turning to dig in a box bolted to the wall.

Brianna wasn't sure exactly what she'd expected; she wasn't even sure what her imago was, not really, beyond the thing that made her look *this* way rather than any other. Not that she herself had had that many options to choose from; she'd been barely 26 when she died, embarrassing in and of itself in a culture where several hundred was the expected lifespan. So 26 she looked still, even after those 150 years of bumming semi-aimlessly round the City.

The thing Dave pulled out was small, and round, and made of a matt blue-grey metal. Dave rested it carefully on top of her head, and she felt a gentle vibration, then a series of tiny prickles across her scalp. Dave let go and stepped back, and she moved her head experimentally. The metal ball stayed where it was, and there was a gentle tugging from each of the prickles.

'Don't touch it,' Dave warned, and she brought her hands back to her lap.

'Close your eyes,' he directed her. 'Close your eyes and tell me exactly what you want these wings to look like. Detail. Detail is good.'

She was hesitant at first, but Dave made encouraging noises every time she stopped, and she found her mental picture getting steadily clearer. At the same time, she started to feel a rising nausea in the pit of her stomach. She swallowed and did her best to ignore it. Then, suddenly, the tone of the box's buzz changed. There was a moment where the prickles in her scalp seemed suddenly tighter, and then they were driving into her skull, and her stomach clenched and seemed to rise up inside her. She fell forwards, retching uncontrollably, and passed out.

She woke up and coughed, bracing for more of the same, before she realised that it had stopped. Dave was gone, and the room was empty, with no sign that she'd ever been ill. Her head felt strangely light, and she put a cautious hand up to confirm that the device had gone. There was a strange sensation in the back of her shoulder-blades. She nearly cricked her neck turning round to see – but there they were, unfurling as she thought about them. Wings.

Brianna had never really outgrown the impetuousness that had got her killed in her first life. She sat up, stepped to the edge of the veranda, and launched herself off into the blue.

Somewhat to her surprise, when she returned to Dave's after that first heady flight, her shoulder-bag was still there, although it no longer fit across her back. She transferred the change of clothes and her lucky frog to a new kit that strapped across her hip; bought a few weeks of dried provisions and instructions on how to get water from the rain-farms dotted across Cerulean's sky; and set off, out into the emptiness.

She spent the first few days playing with her new abilities, testing wind currents, heading steadily away from Cerulean Groundbound and into clear, open, *empty* sky. By the third day there was nothing and no one in view anywhere around her. She felt something relax in her shoulders for the first time since she'd run.

The day after that, halfway through attempting a somersault, she felt a twinge in her left wing. She straightened out from the somersault, and wriggled her shoulders, trying to shake the awkwardness out. Something moved below her feet, and she looked down to see a feather spiralling downwards. Feathers, she supposed, must moult occasionally. But then the itch in her wings intensified, and spread, and she saw another couple of feathers spiralling after the first.

Permanent, Dave had said. Permanent, according to that shifty-eyed bloke in the hostel who hadn't told her what *he'd* had done.

Another handful of feathers. Her stomach lurched as she started to list downwards on one side. Her shoulder-blades were beginning to ache now, as well, and she could hear a creak in the big, light bones of her wings. She tried to spread her wings wider, to hold her position in the sky, and felt herself instead dropping downwards. A cloud loomed underneath her, and by the time she'd come out through the bottom of it, her drift downwards had become a plummet. She glanced over her shoulder to see the final disintegration of her wings.

She'd always hated falling. Not that she had much other option right now. She still wouldn't be able to hurt herself, she supposed, whatever happened when she hit – the ground? Cerulean didn't *have* any ground. When she hit the bottom of the District? What would happen then? Would she just stop? How did the boundless sky of Cerulean finish, at the bottom of the City?

'Well, that'll be something new,' she said aloud.

She set her teeth and straightened herself out, doing her best, without wings, to surf the wind that whistled past her. She remembered seeing skydivers in some District or other a few years back. Now here a skydiver really had *scope*. She arrowed herself forwards into the wind and found herself giggling. Might as well make the most of it.

Then, right on the edge of sight, she saw a black speck in the distant below. She narrowed her eyes, trying to make out what could possibly be all the way out here. It was getting bigger with alarming rapidity, and she was headed straight for it. Too big to be another person; too small to be a rain-farm. A ship? Out here?

She thought briefly of altering her course to plummet straight past it – but really, the serendipity was too much to pass up. The huge balloon-sails were getting bigger, and closer...

She bounced off the sails with a noise of resistant nanofibres, slid down part of the rigging, then something tore under her feet and she landed with a stunning thump on the deck. It was a moment before she could collect herself even enough to roll over and open her eyes. As she blinked her brain back into operation, a ring of concerned-looking faces came into focus, peering down at her.

'Are you alright?' a side-eyed collateral asked after a moment.

A superfluous question, here in the City, but one which still seemed to be hardwired into the human(ish) social brain of the majority of its residents.

'A little shaken,' Brianna replied honestly.

Hitting the deck at close to terminal velocity might not *injure*, but it was a little disconcerting nonetheless. She took a fortifying breath and gingerly sat up.

'So,' she asked brightly. 'Where am I?'

The *Questor*, it turned out, was a ship of science. Sort of.

'The Lost Land,' an avian human explained proudly.

She looked like the archetypal professor – the small round glasses were surely an affectation, but the neat jacket and trousers, and the slightly fussy demeanour, probably not. 'They're reputed to appear here – well, we think here – around midsummer. That's why we're all on board.' She gestured round. 'We're all interested in the Lost Land, either as part of our research, as in my case, or as an out-of-work activity. We're all researchers or aficionados of the mythos, and we're here to demonstrate its reality.'

'Or its unreality, Ariadne,' another of the group corrected. 'You need a sceptic along so you don't all just hallucinate the whole thing into existence.'

Ariadne glared at him.

'The Lost Land,' Brianna repeated.

'I expect you've heard the stories,' Ariadne said brightly, turning back to her. 'It features in most avian cultures.'

Brianna couldn't say that she had, but then she hadn't spent that much time in avian cultures. They tended not to be very accessible by the ground-bound. She rubbed at the back of her shoulder-blades.

'Marvellous treasures and hidden secrets,' the side-eyed collateral who had first spoken said, his beak snapping off the end of each word. His furled balloon-pouches fluttered at the edges of his wings.

Ariadne was frowning again. 'I'm sure none of us are motivated by *treasure*, Lenos,' she said reprovingly.

'Speak for yourself.' The mutter came from a young Neanderthal who squatted on the deck a little back from the others, surrounded by a pile of metal objects. He gave Brianna a quick wink, almost hidden by his brow-ridge.

'The trip is worthwhile for science, and historical discovery.' Ariadne again.

'Some of us paid our own shares, *Professor*,' Lenos snapped. 'And there's nothing wrong with looking for a return on that.' He looked down again at Brianna. 'What about the hitch-hiker, then? She hasn't bought in at all.'

Brianna shrugged, stung. 'I can just hop back on over the side.'

Ariadne looked shocked. 'But of course you must stay, dear. To just arrive like this...' She stopped. 'How *did* you arrive?'

'My transport failed,' Brianna said, with precisely no desire to go into the details.

'She can't stay. Not enough provisions.' The person who spoke, eyeing Brianna with unconcealed distrust, was shorter, with lizard-like skin, green and dry-scaled. He shoved his fifth and sixth limbs, set halfway down his torso, into one of the many pockets of his loose vest, but not before Brianna had noticed the scarred lump that stood in for a hand at the end of the right-hand one. It looked surprisingly angry for a resurrected injury.

'Shipwrecked!' Ariadne declared. 'We have a *duty* to help, Arak.'

'We have a *duty* not to run out of food,' Arak said, hands still twitching uncomfortably.

'Ah, look, our illustrious captain approaches,' Lenos said. 'Zie can settle the matter.'

Walking along the deck was another tall, winged, and quite ridiculously attractive posthuman. Zir shoulder-length hair was loosely tied back, showing high cheekbones, and zie had wings of the sort that Brianna had seen on religious paintings in a Renaissance District a few years back.

The rest of the crew made room, and zie stopped and smiled down at Brianna.

'So,' zie said, offering her a hand. 'A visitor!'

'I just dropped in,' Brianna said, hating herself slightly for the inanity, but the posthuman's smile broadened further – yup, that qualified as 'dazzling' alright – in apparent delight.

She took the offered hand – someone's fingers lingered just a little longer than was necessary, but she wasn't entirely sure whose – and was pulled to her feet without apparent effort.

'Welcome on board! I am Tzeki, the captain of this fine vessel. And you are already making the acquaintance of the rest of our crew.'

'Brianna,' she introduced herself.

'May I ask if this is merely a passing visit?'

'She can't stay,' Arak said forcefully, just as Ariadne said, 'I have offered her our hospitality.'

They glared at each other.

'Arak, so ungenerous!' Tzeki said. 'One more will hardly stretch our resources.'

'We've had each other's company for weeks,' someone else said from the back of the group. 'I'd say we could use a little fresh blood.'

'She doesn't get any shares in anything we find,' Lenos said.

'Of course not,' Brianna agreed.

'Then that is settled,' Tzeki said firmly. 'Brianna, it is a pleasure, and we must talk later.' Zie gave her another of those smiles, then turned away. 'For now, Professor, Arak, a word, if I may.'

Zie drew Ariadne off up the deck. Arak followed them, after a quick glance back at Brianna and another pat of his pockets. The rest of the crew began to drift away, but the Neanderthal who had winked at her earlier stayed put, looking at her a little quizzically.

'Charles,' he said, nodding at her. 'Pleasure to see a new face.'

Brianna, suddenly tired again, sat down on a coil of rope opposite him.

'Don't mind Arak,' he added. 'Engine trouble last night. Bit irritable today.'

'So Arak's the engineer, then?' Brianna asked.

'Good, too,' Charles said. 'Nearly didn't have him. Captain and engineer up and left, day before we sailed.' He sniffed. 'Paid 'em already, too. Bastards. Said we were a bunch of loonies who couldn't even decide when midsummer was and fucked off. Not got the skills to leave without them. Thought the whole thing was over. Tzeki and Arak showed up next day. Saved the expedition.' He looked down at the piece of metal he was cleaning. 'Saved us a lot of money, too, if we'd had to abort.'

'Wow,' Brianna said. That sounded like a hell of a coincidence to her, even if Charles seemed to think nothing of it. Then again, he was sailing around the middle of nowhere looking for a mythical Lost Land, so perhaps not the most reliable of witnesses.

'How d'you get here, then?' he asked suddenly, looking at her sharply.

Brianna hesitated for a moment. 'Transport fail,' she said again.

'Dinghy dumped you out?' Charles said. 'Shitty engines. Arak's teaching me engines.' He tossed the piece of metal onto a pile next to him, and took another out of a bag.

'How long have you been out here? And what did you mean about midsummer?' Brianna asked.

'Bout four weeks,' Charles said. 'Running out of time, really. Thing is, right, when's midsummer, in a place with no proper star-sun? Not like it's actually Cerulean where most of the legends started, either. When's their midsummer? Best guess, is all we've got. Best District to look. Best time to look. Implications and rumours. A week, at most, before we've missed it for this year.' He sighed. 'A lot of us counting on it, too. Expensive business, kitting out a ship.' He chewed briefly at his lip. 'No chute backup, then, in your dinghy?'

'Fucking rip-off merchants, back at Groundbound,' Brianna agreed vaguely, then got to her feet, not wanting to answer any more questions. Charles threw another piece of metal into the 'clean' pile, and stood up too.

'Best go give Arak this lot. See you later.' He scooped them up and wandered off.

She looked around, wanting to speak to more of the crew; find out more about what they were doing and about the whole Lost Land thing. But no one else was in sight, and most unusually for her, she felt slightly loath just to dive in and go looking. Her shoulders sagged, and she realised that she was suddenly, excruciatingly, tired. The aftermath of the endorphin rush, she supposed. She wandered idly around the edge of the ship, nodding slightly timidly at Lenos when she passed him fiddling with some of the rigging, until she found a hammock on the port side deck, slung underneath the stairs that led up to the upper deck. She was almost dozing off when she heard tinny voices close to her ear. She jumped, then noticed a ventilation grate a little above the hammock.

'Shut the door, for pity's sake,' one of the voices said irritably. 'Let's not have this discussion where the whole crew can hear.'

'I am certain that you are overreacting.' Tinny or not, that was definitely Tzeki. Brianna pricked up her ears.

'Nonsense.'

The other voice sounded like Arak, the engineer. There was a creaking noise, and Brianna couldn't catch the next few words, before Arak's voice was suddenly clear again. '...And what the hell is that outlander Brianna doing here?'

All she caught of Tzeki's response was '...all outlanders here... sure it is nothing.'

'It better had be nothing.' Arak sounded clearer again now. 'And what if this damn land doesn't show up? What then? We'd be safer without her, anyway.'

'Arak, you are overreacting,' Tzeki's voice was low but clear. 'And if it does not appear, we will think of another solution.'

Arak made a mistrusting noise, but after that both of their voices died away quietly, and she heard nothing more before a door finally slammed.

Well now.

Cerulean was one of the Districts with a local sun, but with no real horizon, it never exactly set. The light just gradually faded from the sky, starting at the places furthest from the glowing, distant sun. Brianna leant on the ship's rail and watched the light shrink in on itself, coalescing around the shining ball of the sun.

Ariadne had found her on the hammock, and given her a half-hour lecture on the Lost Land, delivered as though Brianna were one of her slower students. Once she'd escaped that, she'd wandered around the ship a little, watching the crew doing their thing. There was something she found deeply admirable about their focus; the way that despite the odd internal tension they were pulling together. She sighed a little wistfully. All of them shared the same light in their eyes when they talked about the Land. Some people might have called it obsession. Brianna didn't think she'd ever been obsessed with anything. Or even – she pushed away the recollection of that house halfway across the City – all that committed.

The sun sank further beneath the ship, and shadows pooled deeply around her on the deck. Idly, she held a hand out over the side and saw her palm light up with the reflected glow from the sun beneath. She leant over a little to see sunlight still glinting off the side-planks of the ship, then a little more, squinting downwards at the inwards curve of the ship's underside.

She was just craning to see the ship's keel – did airships even have keels? – when the back of her neck prickled. Someone behind her? She began to lean back inboard and turn to see, but it was too late – a hard shove between her shoulder-blades and her right knee grabbed and lifted, and she was tumbling overboard.

She grabbed out blindly as she fell, her hand bouncing off something she couldn't quite get hold of, then threw her arms forwards as her feet flipped over her head, trying desperately to push herself into the side of the ship. The second time her hand hit something, she just managed to grab it. She very nearly lost her grip again at the jerk on her shoulder when the rest of her cannoned into the ship. She brought her other hand up to grab the same bit of sticky-feeling rope, then hung there for a moment, breathing hard.

The light was nearly gone now, but there was enough to show her the unpromising outlook. She was holding onto a piece of rope tied to an embedded iron loop; but looking along and up, the ship's sides were slick and bare. About three metres to her right there was an access ladder leading upwards, but she could no more reach it than she could, lacking those damn wings she'd paid so much for, fly back up to the deck.

'Help!' she called experimentally, but the deck had been empty before she fell and she had no reason to suppose that anyone was there now. Other than whoever had pushed her, and it seemed pretty unlikely that they would decide to rescue her at this point.

'Help!'

She hung there for a while, cursing, in no particular order, herself for not paying more attention, the mysterious person doing the pushing, and the situation as a whole. The rope was, very gradually, slipping through her hands. Oh well. It looked like Plan A, falling straight through the District, was back on. She sighed again, and wiggled a little, preparing to let go.

'Brianna!'

Or not.

'Down here!'

Tzeki swept down, lit from below by the last embers of the sun, glowing across zir arms and shoulders. Zie hovered behind her.

'If I may just take you by the waist,' zie said politely, and Brianna couldn't stifle a slightly hysterical giggle.

Then they were soaring back upwards to land on the deck. The ship's lights were lit now, dispelling the earlier pools of shadows, and half the crew were clustered round, twittering anxiously over her as she and Tzeki landed, and the sudden moment of wondering how Tzeki had known how to show up and find her fell away.

* * *

Tzeki stayed solicitously by her through dinner, and afterwards, offered to give her a tour of the ship. Happily, this gave Brianna scope both to further investigate what zie and Arak might be up to, and to flirt like hell.

'Aren't you on duty or something?' she asked.

'Ah, no, the Professor is on the bridge. I need only be contactable,' zie tapped zir comm, 'in case of anything untoward.' Zie bowed slightly to her, smiled, and offered an arm to escort her along the deck. 'I confess that I rather hope that no such happens in the next little while.'

All it took in the end was a few more, increasingly pointed, innuendos from both of them, and then a suggestion from Brianna that she might quite like to see the captain's accommodation. Which was spartan but quite accommodating, particularly in the bed area.

'Spacious,' Brianna said approvingly, and got down to the important business of investigating what Tzeki wasn't already showing off under that vest.

Things were progressing quite satisfactorily when there was a frantic rattling of the doorhandle, and Tzeki sat up in alarm, grabbing at zir comm.

'Tzeki!'

Bloody Arak again.

'Is something wrong?' Tzeki asked. 'But the bridge...'

'What do you think you're doing?' On the last word, Arak obviously lost patience, and the door splintered around the lock and opened.

'What do you think *you're* doing?' she demanded, far too annoyed to make any pretence at embarrassment.

Arak waved a wild finger at her. 'You! I don't believe for a second this is just coincidence! In the middle of nowhere! Zie hasn't got it and zie wouldn't give it to you anyway!'

'Hasn't got what?' Brianna demanded testily. 'I'm not here,' she pointed at the bed, 'to get anything apart from laid, you scaly moron. Now get the hell out so we can get on with it.'

Arak turned to Tzeki. 'There was someone after us at the port. Now she shows up in the middle of nowhere. They've been tracking us! They want it back! They want *me*!'

Tzeki said, more loudly this time. 'Arak! Stop! I am sure that Brianna is not what you think.'

'But how do you know?' Arak demanded, eyes wild. 'We're taking too much of a risk!'

Tzeki, finally, frowned. 'Arak, I do not wish to say this, but – whose was the risk, at the start? You go too far. You will calm yourself now.'

Something, finally, seemed to get through to Arak. He opened his mouth, then shut it again, breathing hard.

Brianna considered the option of remaining pissed off herself, but she badly wanted to know what the hell was going on, and being a little conciliatory had a higher chance of achieving that.

'Is there anything I could do that would prove that I'm not – whatever it is that you think I am?' she asked, wrapping the sheet around her.

'You could explain how the hell you got here, for starters,' Arak said, eyeing her narrowly.

Brianna sighed. Logically, it wasn't that big of a deal, she supposed. Foolish though she felt about the whole thing. And it didn't sound like either of these two was likely to care all that much about the legality of the situation. She told them, in as few words as possible.

For a long moment afterwards, Arak and Tzeki looked at one another.

'Shit,' Arak said finally, looking away and puffing out a long breath. He patted absently at his pockets again.

'It is too late,' Tzeki agreed quietly.

'Too late for what?' Brianna asked.

'I heard some of the same rumours as you,' Arak said, turning back to face her. 'I wasn't interested for myself, but... well, anyway, I went looking. It sounds like you got lucky; someone with the same tech, but some kind of ethics.' He shrugged. 'The people I ran into – weren't like that.'

He glanced down at the stump where his hand wasn't, and Brianna's eyebrows rose.

'That was from *here*? It didn't happen in the Universe?'

It hadn't occurred to her until that moment that if you could change someone's imago voluntarily, maybe you could also change it against their will.

Arak shook his head. 'They weren't enthusiastic about me investigating,' he said, and swallowed. 'Tzeki got me out, in the end, before they did anything else. They said they'd start slowly. I... didn't want to leave anything behind, that it could be used against someone else. So I took it, before we left.' He shrugged. 'I thought, from what they said, that maybe that was it. The prototype. The only one.'

'And you figured that they might be quite keen to get their property back,' Brianna concluded.

Arak grimaced. 'I know they are. There's a price out; on the tech, mostly, but on me too.'

'You see then,' Tzeki said, 'why Arak was so concerned by your coincidental arrival.'

'But why are you both on the run, if it's him they're after?' Brianna demanded.

Tzeki shrugged, and Brianna lost concentration for a moment in admiring the play of muscle across zir shoulders. 'He is from my deme.'

Brianna blinked. 'I wouldn't go on the lam with a bunch of psychopaths after me for anyone from *my* deme.'

'Perhaps yours are less close,' Tzeki agreed.

Brianna's chest ached slightly. She didn't think she'd ever been that close to someone, platonically or romantically or any other damn way. If she'd felt like that about Clara, she wouldn't be here, halfway across the City, on the run from herself and the consequences of her actions.

'So what are you doing here?' Brianna asked. 'Just somewhere a long, long way away?'

'Initially, Cerulean seemed sufficiently far distant for us to stop for a while,' Tzeki said. 'But Arak saw someone near the station, and we needed after all to move on. I overheard some of the crew of this ship talking of their voyage, and it seemed like an ideal opportunity.'

'The captain and engineer didn't even need much of a bribe,' Arak noted.

'And then,' Tzeki said, 'we thought: the Lost Land – it is *lost*. Even if we find it, afterwards it will again be lost. Where else to dispose of something you do not wish to be found?'

'Can't you just,' she waved a hand, 'get rid of it?'

Arak shook his head. 'I tried. Not with anything we have access to.' He sighed, and scrubbed one of his hands over his face. 'Not that there's any point any more, I guess.'

'You must still get rid of it,' Tzeki said. 'Both for your safety, and for your wellbeing.'

Brianna frowned. 'Anyway. What Dave did didn't exactly last long. If what you have is permanent, maybe whatever he's got is –' she waved a hand, '– a knockoff. Still worth getting rid of what you took, I mean.'

Arak shrugged and got to his feet. 'Yes. Well. We'll see.'

He went to the door, and said without turning round. 'I'll leave you to it. I'm sorry I interrupted.'

Brianna badly wanted to interrogate Tzeki more about the whole situation. But slightly more than that, she wanted to return to where they left off. Other things could wait.

She offered, the next morning, to help out with whatever chores needed doing, motivated in part by a wish to do a little more investigating, and in part by a less-acknowledged wish to join in. Lenos was more than happy to recruit her.

'Although,' he said slightly doubtfully, 'it's usually the avian types who do this.'

'I'll be fine,' Brianna said.

Halfway up one of the swaying masts, on her way to repair the balloon-sail that she had crashed through the previous day, she was slightly regretting her rashness. She glanced downwards, and had a momentary dizzying flashback to the previous evening. She took a deep breath, loosened her panicked grip a little, and began to run the patch-gun carefully over the edges of the rip. If it hadn't been Arak, who had it been? A sudden gust rattled the rigging, and in managing not to drop the patch-gun, she let the speculation go again.

She got back to the deck to an approving pat on the back from Lenos, and looked round for someone else to help, or possibly to interrogate. Charles was sitting on a couple of boxes, carefully cleaning off bits of engine.

'Engine pieces from Arak,' he explained, handing her a piece of machinery and a rag that smelt slightly peculiar. 'Spare prop – swapped in last week for a while. Bird stuck in the main one.'

Brianna turned the piece over gingerly, looking for signs of dead bird.

'No, no,' Charles said cheerfully. 'Went in afterwards. Main one's sorted and back in now. Just cleaning this up for the spares pile.'

Brianna hadn't quite appreciated the depth of Charles' interest in engines. She tuned out a little as he told her about propellers.

'Strange bloke, Arak,' he said, suddenly. 'Something on his mind, I reckon.'

'Yeah?' Brianna said.

Charles shrugged. 'Bit distracted, sometimes. Wonder what it is.'

'I don't think I've been here long enough to notice, really,' Brianna said.

'Saw you hanging out with Tzeki,' Charles said. 'Thought you might know more about how they showed up here.'

'We didn't really discuss it,' Brianna said.

Charles shrugged. 'Sure. Just – bit odd. Them showing up last minute. You falling onto the ship.'

Brianna blinked. 'Hey, I'm not the one out here sailing in circles looking for a legend,' she said lightly, but Charles was still eyeing her slightly oddly.

Could Charles have pushed her? Why?

'True,' he said after a moment, and looked down again. 'Suppose it's all a bit odd, really.'

They worked in silence for a moment longer, before Charles began to talk again about the details of the engine. Brianna's discomfort mostly faded, but after a little longer, she made an excuse and wandered off to the other side of the ship.

She made her way up to the side deck off the bridge and leant over the rail, watching the crew moving around below. Charles was still fiddling with engine parts. Surely, if Arak and Tzeki had come on board at such short notice, no one currently in the crew could be after them? They'd all been committed long before.

'Land! Land!'

Her head jerked upwards. The Professor, standing at the bridge over the wheel, was pointing off the starboard bow, and there in the distance, something was glistening. For a moment, the crew were all still, all staring over that rail.

'Hard starboard!' Tzeki called. The Professor was already spinning the wheel. Lenos, wings spread, dropped down from somewhere up in the rigging and began shouting orders. People ran to the ropes, and their speed picked up as the balloon-sails shifted position.

It looked almost like a mirage, a rough-edged round bubble on the horizon, drawing almost too rapidly closer as the frenetic activity on deck intensified. The details were indistinct; a sandy shore rising into gentle wooded hills. Exactly in the centre something rose much taller – Brianna squinted but couldn't quite make it out. A tower? Were there humans there already, then, or had there been once? The Professor had straightened up the wheel, but even from halfway across the ship, Brianna could see the tension in her hands as she clutched it and stared fiercely towards the Land.

They were nearly there now. Except – Brianna blinked. Was it shimmering more? It still looked solid, but...

'It's fading!' Lenos cried in anguish. He was at the rail closest to it, wings spread and hovering slightly off the floor, as though he was seriously considering throwing himself off the ship and towards it.

The Land was wavering around the edges, the air around it shaking. Brianna could feel a wind beginning to whip at her hair.

'Lenos, no!' someone called. 'The wind's too strong.'

'Too late,' Brianna whispered. 'We found it too late.'

'The lifeboats!' the Professor shouted over the increasing noise of the wind. 'We can still reach it by boat.'

Charles, below, was fumbling at the ropes that secured the lifeboat pulleys. Lenos had abandoned the idea of flying across, and instead had pushed his way to the front of the group crowding round the rail to clamber over into the lifeboat.

The wind was increasing further now, and Brianna saw the edges of the Land begin to turn, the whole thing starting to spiral into a vortex. She began to feel a pull, and the ship shuddered under her.

'A tornado,' Tzeki said calmly. 'We must leave now, or be pulled apart. Hard port, if you please.'

'But...!' the Professor wailed.

'Now,' Tzeki insisted implacably, taking the wheel from her and spinning it back to port.

The ship began to turn slowly away from the Land, juddering, the sails flapping madly with Lenos still by the lifeboat and paying them no attention. Tzeki, handing the wheel back to Ariadne, balanced on a rail at the other side of the bridge and called down to one of the few crew-members not scrambling round the lifeboat.

Arak, still on the deck just below Brianna, was fumbling desperately in one of his many pockets, and suddenly she saw something in his hand, round, matt blue-grey... For a moment, she heard someone telling her to think hard about her wings, then felt the echo of a phantom nausea that had her dry-retching for a moment.

Further up the ship, by the lifeboat, Charles looked down the deck towards Arak, and dropped the pulley rope. There was a clatter, and one end of the lifeboat dropped like a stone. The burly human on the other pulley held it for a moment, then let go, falling backwards, and Brianna saw the lifeboat whipped away from the side of the ship. It danced in the wind for a moment before being pulled into the tornado, pieces flying off it. Lenos, halfway over the side into it, was being hauled back into the ship, but Charles was running down the ship's side towards Arak.

'Mine!' he howled, and Arak turned, his eyes widening.

Charles was on him before he could react, pinning him to the ship's rail and grappling for the imago-device. Arak glanced over his shoulder for a moment; the tornado was still whipping its edges towards them, but it was beginning to recede as Tzeki's efforts to pull the sails round paid off. Brianna could hear the engine screaming in tandem with the wind whipping through the rigging. Arak's eyes were desperate now, as he tried to turn, to bring an arm up... To throw it, Brianna realised. He was trying to throw it into the tornado that had been the Lost Land, but Charles still had him pinned against the rail, and while Arak was keeping the imago-device away from Charles, he couldn't turn enough to throw it and he couldn't pass it to his damaged middle arm.

He looked up.

'Brianna!' he called. His other middle arm whipped up and over, and the imago-device came tumbling through the air towards her.

For a moment, she held it in her hands. For a moment, she considered keeping it. If it really was the same technology that Dave had used, maybe she could get her wings back... permanently, even, this time...

Then she turned, and threw it overhand, as hard as she could, into the heart of the tornado now screaming where the Lost Land had been a few moments before.

For a moment, she thought she'd missed; that it was falling through the tornado's edge. Arak, craning his neck below her, gasped and reached out with his scarred arm; Charles, still pinning him against the rail, was frozen, watching it fall. Then it was pulled inwards, towards the centre of the Land, and out of sight behind the frantic whipping, turning sand.

Arak relaxed against the rail, and Charles screamed and grabbed him by the shoulders, lifting him off his feet and pushing him backwards, halfway over the rail...

Brianna acted without thinking. The drop to the deck below was only a couple of metres; barely enough to do yourself serious damage even back in the Universe. She swung herself over the railing, balanced on the edge for a moment, then launched herself to land directly on top of Charles, grabbing at Arak's shoulder herself as she landed.

Brianna and Charles fell into a crumpled heap on the deck, and a moment later, Arak landed beside them, coughing. For a moment, Charles continued to struggle underneath her, and all her attention was occupied in remaining where she was; then he relaxed and began to sob.

'Shit, the engine,' she heard Arak say, from what seemed like a great distance away, and she heard his footsteps unsteadily staggering across the deck to the engine-room hatch.

She supposed she should do something about Charles, but for now, she couldn't quite cope with moving. She lay on top of Charles, who was still weeping, and listened to Tzeki calling more orders, and to the change in the engine-noise thrumming through the deck, and to the tornado-wind dying away, and waited for someone to come and sort everything out.

Brianna sat down beside Arak on the steps that led down to the engine-room.

'Well,' she said.

'Either it's ripped apart, or it's safely on the Land,' Arak said.

'Maybe you can come back and check sometime,' Brianna said lightly.

'Ha.'

There was a pause.

'It was too late, already,' Arak said. 'It's out there. Your Dave won't be the only one. Even if it's just knockoffs now, someone'll work it out sooner or later.'

'Yes,' Brianna agreed. 'Doesn't mean you weren't doing the right thing, though.' She paused. 'Was Charles after the thing, or you?'

'Either,' Arak said. 'Both. He needed the money. Bankrupted himself with this. He said that when they first approached him, just before we sailed, he said no. But then when we couldn't reach the Land... I think he'd have settled for the device, but once that was gone, he figured that getting rid of me would be worth something.' He shrugged. 'Poor bloke. I get the impression he had to borrow quite a lot to be here.' He looked over at her. 'It was him, pushed you over. He thought the same as me, that you were after it too.'

'Does that mean you're in danger back at Groundbound?' Brianna asked.

'I will deal with it,' Tzeki said, appearing behind them. 'There is little for them to gain, now. I will deal with it.'

Arak shrugged. 'Let's hope so, eh?'

The three of them sat for a while longer in silence, watching the shadows lengthen as the sun sank beneath the ship. Brianna leaned her head back against Tzeki, and thought about belonging, and support, and other things.

'So,' she asked. 'What are you two up to now? Once we're back in port and you've dealt with Arak's little problem.'

'I'm kind of enjoying the engineering, actually. And Cerulean. I like it here,' Arak said. 'I think maybe we might look for another ship in need of crew.'

'Room for a third?' Brianna found herself asking. She felt Tzeki's smile in zir chest, and Arak looked over at her, cocking his head to one side briefly, then looked down again.

'You'd better pay a bit more attention to me than you did to Charles when you want to know about engines, then,' he said.

Brianna grinned, and watched the colours playing across the sky. Cerulean might not a bad place to be, for the next little while. And after that – well, she'd see.

HIGHBURY

Helen Angove

A gentleman should be allowed to consider a library a place of refuge: a room where he can have the reasonable expectation of temporary retreat from the distractions of domestic life and the interruptions of the fairer sex. It so happened, however, that the Misses Maitland had been in occupation of the library for the past half-hour. Anxious to improve their minds, they were engaged in the creditable and becoming exercise of drawing up a reading list.

'This one!' cried Sophia. 'Regard the title!'

She had removed from the shelf a calf-bound volume. *'The Human Species: a Spotter's Guide*, by Dr Melicia Clutterbuck,' she read. 'I am certain Papa could find nothing objectionable in *this* one.'

'But it is *Papa's* library,' replied her elder sister. 'He would not have anything in his own library that *he* would consider unsuitable. But what of Mamma?'

'Oh! Mamma will not object if Papa does not.'

'But the refinement of your mind, Sophy! You would not wish to be thought coarse.'

Of the two sisters, it was Miss Maitland who was usually considered the greater beauty. She was tall and well formed, with a fair complexion. Miss Sophia, on the other hand, had freckles and red hair, yet her figure had a pleasing elasticity and her face an animation wholly lacking in that of her sister. In character they were as little alike as they were in appearance, but both were generally considered good-natured, accomplished young women.

'I hardly know *what* I wish for!' replied Sophia, throwing herself down onto the settle. 'It is all very well for you, Maria. Your life will change soon enough, and there will be variety and enjoyment enough for *you*. I am to remain here in Highbury District, and be dull.'

'It is by no means certain that my marriage will take place so soon as you imagine,' replied Maria. 'John has not yet concluded his business in the Romuline, and there is no guarantee that it will be finished soon.'

'How can you be so calm!' cried her sister. 'I am sure I should not be so, in your place. Although if Papa has his will, I never *shall* be in your place. How am I to meet young men if Papa will never allow us to travel?'

'There is Captain Wainwright. Mamma would not have invited him to stay had she not believed him in every way to be a respectable young man.'

'Captain Wainwright is a very pleasing young man, I am sure, but I do not see how I could attach myself to a man who has swim bladder and gills, be he ever so eligible. Besides, he is looking to purchase an estate here, and I would not wish to be settled in Highbury all my afterlife.'

'Mr Davenport, then.'

'Captain Wainwright's friend?'

'The same. *He* has no gills.'

'Is he of independent means?'

'I believe so.'

'His appearance is not without distinction. I shall consider the matter.'

'But we are not here to gossip. We should be reading,' said Miss Maitland, taking the book from the hands of her younger sister. She opened it, letting the pages fall as they would, and began—

'Cro-Magnon man, early Homo sapiens sapiens,*' she read, 'are physically little distinguished from their descendants. However, mitochondrial DNA sequencing has shown that...'*

'Dear me, Maria! I shall die of boredom if you have the choosing of the text! Give *me* the book!' And without waiting for a response, Sophia reclaimed the book, opened it to a fresh page, and continued—

'It is the wont of those human sub-species of more straightforward human descent to regard the Ettin, Homo phobovore, *with some suspicion: the more so, perhaps, because they are physically indistinguishable from so many other human*

species. Ah! *This* is more interesting, Maria! *Although the species has classically been understood to 'feed' on fear, this is not the exact truth. Rather, it is the telepathic detection of strong emotion in another that stimulates the relevant nerve centres of the creature's brain, producing a strong pleasure response, comparable almost to the experience of orgasm. Whilst the...'*

'Sophy! I am surprised at you! Surely even *you* cannot imagine that this is a suitable passage for a young lady,' cried Maria.

Sophia made a sound of impatience, but leafed through the pages of the book once more.

'Abarimon,' she read. *'The Abarimon,* Homo abarimoniensis, *are adapted to thin atmospheres in which most human racial types would be unable to survive. Physically they are of unremarkable appearance, save for their feet, which appear to point backwards compared to the usual human norm, but despite—or perhaps because of—this handicap they are able to run at great speeds. Culturally they are often described as primitive, and are rarely seen to wear clothes...'*

'Sophy! This book has illustrations, has it not?'

'Yes, Maria.'

'And the illustration on this page: would you consider it suitable for the eyes of a young lady?'

'Oh I grow tired of this!' cried Sophia. 'As soon as I find something—anything—of interest in a volume, you tell me that it is unsuitable, or unseemly, or vulgar and forbid me to read it!'

Miss Maitland was saved the trouble of replying by the opening of the library door. A footman entered. 'Your mother is asking for you, Miss Maitland,' he announced.

'Thank you, James,' replied Maria. 'Sophy, I must go to Mamma, but I wish you would refrain from reading any more of that book whilst I am gone.'

'And who are *you*, pray, to give orders to me, Maria!' The words were spoken with some attempt at composure, but there was no doubt of the strength of the feeling behind them. However, the rustle of Miss Maitland's skirt as she swept from the room was all the satisfaction Sophia received.

Perhaps the reader can imagine the relief with which I watched Miss Maitland depart. The two young ladies had been completely unaware of any other presence in the library, hidden as I was in a wing chair in the shadows of a corner: now the eldest sister had left, I hoped fervently that the younger might soon follow. And I might yet have escaped detection altogether had not my gaze happened to light upon the servant's face, and had not my attention been caught by something slightly odd in the set of his features. It was enough: although largely hidden from the gaze of the young ladies I was easily visible from where the servant stood by the door, and noticing my gaze, he addressed me. 'Do you have enough light with which to read, sir?' he asked. 'Shall I fetch a candle?'

The acuteness of my embarrassment can only be imagined: compounded of course, by the immediate transferral of Sophia's attention from the departure of her sister. 'Why, Mr Davenport! I do believe you have been spying upon us! You sly thing!'

'No indeed, Miss Sophia. I would not dream...'

'For shame, Mr Davenport. I declare you are blushing!'

'I would not have intruded... indeed, I had assumed you to already be aware of my presence...' But that was a lie, and she knew it. The truth was that I had already been in the library at the arrival of Sophia and her sister, and had been too embarrassed to declare myself. Now I was to pay the price in the endurance of Sophia's flirtatiousness.

I rose to take my leave. If the library was to prove no refuge, residence in the Maitland household was likely to prove more trying than I had anticipated. I was already finding the perpetual atmosphere of repressed emotion somewhat wearing.

I had only come to Highbury out of a kind of vague academic interest (I had read English Literature back in 21st-century Cambridge) and at the desire for company of my friend

Captain Henry Wainwright, a single man in possession of a good fortune who was indeed in search of a wife. Wainwright was hoping that—in the rarefied atmosphere of Highbury, a District populated almost entirely by Jane Austen enthusiasts or people actually of the Regency period of England—his naval background and wealth might count for more, and his posthuman marine adaptations count for less than they seemed to do in the wider city. Sophia's attitude would seem to suggest otherwise, but I had not had the heart to tell him so, especially given the pains he had taken to secure us the proper introductions into Highbury society.

The presence of Captain Wainwright and myself in the house had prompted the Maitlands to invite others of their acquaintance to dine, among them Lady Horatia Warrington. We were given to understand that her presence amongst us was a great honour: not only was she the principal resident of the immediate area, but she was also Council Member for Highbury District. Her voice dominated the room as we rejoined the ladies in the drawing room after dinner.

'I hope, Mrs Maitland, that we are to have entertainment tonight. A truly elegant gathering *must* comprise entertainment.'

Mrs Maitland assured her ladyship that the card tables would be brought out immediately.

'Oh no, Mamma!' cried Sophia. 'I understand that in the best circles card playing is now considered *quite* out of fashion.'

'I declare, you give your opinion with great decision for such a young woman,' responded Lady Horatia.

'I would not have it thought that our hospitality was in any way lacking,' replied Sophia. She raised her eyes to meet those of the older woman, and held her gaze. It may be that I did not admire Sophia's coquetry, but, at that moment, I was impressed by her assurance.

The momentary silence was broken by Captain Wainwright. 'Perhaps, then, Miss Sophia would be good enough to play the pianoforte for us,' he cried. The Captain knew well enough that it was the desire to exhibit her accomplishments that lay behind Sophia's professed distaste for cards. If he had hoped to obtain her goodwill in this manner he was disappointed, however, for whilst Sophia sat at the instrument with alacrity enough, it was towards *me* that she looked for help to turn the pages of her music.

'If you would be so kind, Mr Davenport?' she murmured.

'Indeed, Miss Sophia, I would, with the greatest of pleasure, but I am no musician,' I responded, disconcerted.

'You do yourself an injustice, Mr Davenport, I am sure.'

'Captain Wainwright is a most superior musician, let Captain Wainwright be your aide, he will be of far more use than I.'

'Why, Mr Davenport,' she responded archly, 'I do believe you are reluctant to put yourself forward in company. But we are all friends here, you see. You need not be shy.'

Bowing to the inevitable, I made my way to the pianoforte, avoiding the accusing eyes of my friend. I hoped only that my meagre skill in following a musical score would be enough to enable me to turn the pages in the correct places, and Sophia's musicianship sufficiently accomplished to make up for any deficiencies. I took my place at her right hand, and peered at the sheet music in the candlelight.

She began to play a Beethoven sonata, and I was surprised to discover that she played excellently: not just with technical accuracy, but with subtlety and real feeling. Subtlety had not been, up until that point, a virtue that I had associated with Miss Sophia Maitland. Even the footman and butler, I could not help but notice, were listening to her rendition with rapt intensity.

She may have been playing well: but there was a sort of repressed anger in her interpretation of the piece, and she also played fast. I started to follow the score—became lost—found my place again just in time to catch Sophia's pointed nod—turned the page. But the relief at having negotiated that first hurdle made me negligent and I only belatedly returned my eyes to the page: and again I was immediately quite lost! With increasing frenzy my eyes scanned the page for any passage that bore resemblance to that which I was hearing, leaning forward until my nose was almost on the paper. It was only then that I realized that Sophia was nodding again, and—given the emphasis of her movement—not for the first time. I lurched forwards, grabbing at the sheet in a panic and somehow, I never quite understood how, succeeded in knocking the candelabrum off the top of the pianoforte whereupon it tumbled into Sophia's lap, spattering her with liquid wax!

The lady screamed, and jumped away from the instrument, but other than that, made remarkably little fuss. Her mother and sister made up the deficiency, however, what with the cries of fear, the smelling salts and the ringing of the bell for cloths and cold water. I was left in a kind of helpless limbo, standing off to the side, waving my hands and reflexively apologising as the assembled company glared their accusations at me.

It was thus, therefore, that I was in a position to see what nobody else could see. Down by the fireplace was kneeling a servant: a scrawny child engaged in making up the fire. Her clothes and general demeanour of trying not to be seen proclaimed her to be one of the lower servants. It was not the relatively unusual occurrence of seeing a scullion here in the drawing room that caught my attention, however: it was rather that, as she witnessed the scene of panic and embarrassment in the room, her face bore the same expression of fixed and hungry intensity as I had seen on the face of the footman in the library. Upon seeing my gaze upon her, however, she gave a tiny squeak of alarm, gathered brush and coal scuttle, and quitted the room.

Sophia was, at length, proclaimed to be none the worse for the shock (she had, of course, been in no other danger), and allowed to retire to change her soiled gown. I flattened myself against the wall as she passed, but was unable to sufficiently efface myself to avoid her glance.

'Why Mr Davenport!' she exclaimed. 'Such lengths to which to go, to win my attention!'

She laughed, enjoying my confusion. Of course she did not believe the candelabrum incident to have been actually deliberate: what *was* clear, however, was that she believed that my awkwardness was due to her attractiveness: due, in short, to my being discomposed by her publicly asserted interest in me.

I sighed. The one benefit the evening's embarrassment might have wrought—for my gaucheness to have repelled Sophia and allowed me a respite from her advances—was obviously not to be.

Once Sophia had left, I was able to retire to the relative anonymity of the shadows at the back of the room, I turned to Wainwright. 'Did you see that?' I asked.

'I could hardly miss it,' he replied coldly.

'No!' I said. I indicated the fireplace. 'The expression on that servant's face when I knocked the candles over! Did you see it? It was... *weird*.' (With Wainwright I could relax my efforts to restrict myself to 19th-century modes of speech.)

But Wainwright had obviously not yet forgiven me: whether for turning Sophia's pages for her, or for spoiling her dress, I wasn't sure. 'No,' he replied flatly, turning his face away.

If Wainwright was not interested in what I had to say, however, somebody else was. Lady Horatia had heard me.

'A *gentleman*, Mr Davenport,' she proclaimed in tones loud enough for the whole company to hear, 'does *not* pass comment on the servants in another gentleman's house.'

There was nothing I could say or do that would ameliorate the humiliations of the evening. As soon as I decently could, I made my excuses and retired.

The Maitlands' house was a large one, and dark, and despite the aid of the candle I carried with me I must, at some point, have missed my way back to my chamber. Eventually it became necessary for me to retrace my steps almost back as far as the drawing room, and in doing so, I passed the dining room, and heard the sounds of sobs issuing from within.

I opened the door. 'Who's there?' I called. 'Is everything—are you all right?'

The sobs ceased abruptly. I took a further step into the room, and beheld a huddled shape by the fireplace. As my steps carried me towards it, the shape moved, and illuminated by the candle, revealed itself to have a face. It was the scullery maid.

'What is the matter?' I asked. But the child just started to sob again, this time more loudly, and hid her face in her hands.

'What's the matter?' I asked again. Then, hoping a different approach might achieve something, 'What's your name?' Silence. 'You can speak to me, you know. I promise you won't get into trouble.'

She sniffed, and raised her head. 'Bessie, sir.'

'Can you tell me what the matter is, Bessie?' I tried to make my voice gentle.

'Nothing.'

'*Something* must be wrong. What are you doing up here anyway? Surely this is a parlour maid's job?'

The servant let out a wail, and had to compose herself before she was able to answer. 'The under parlour maid has eloped with the second gardener,' she forced out, between sobs.

'Oh, I see. So you are having to do her work as well as your own?'

The servant nodded.

'And it is too much? You are overworked?'

The maid mumbled something I could not catch. 'I'm sorry?' I asked.

'No sir. Well, yes sir, but... but...' She was crying too hard to finish.

'Then what *is* the matter?'

'I am so... so rarely above stairs, sir! And then—and then—you *saw* me!'

'I don't understand.'

'You saw me and I had to leave the room! A lower servant should not be *seen*, sir! And I so need—I so desire—to be above stairs!'

'Oh. Oh dear, I'm sorry. But—I don't see—'

'You wouldn't understand.' The girl spoke in terms of finality, and, wiping her eyes with the back of her hand, gave another huge sniff, picked up the coal scuttle, and left the room.

The following day found me, after the embarrassments and confusions of the previous day, anxious, if at all possible, to avoid company. Breakfast, of course, had to be endured: but following this I declined my host's offer of joining them to shoot, and expressed a desire to fish instead. This, apparently, was an acceptable request, and I went in search of the head gardener, who I was told would furnish me with tackle.

The head gardener was very obliging. Not only did he supply the necessary equipment, but was also good enough to point me in the direction of a spot on the banks of the stream that was, he said, a favourite of Mr Maitland's.

When I reached it, I could see why. Although within only a few feet of the apparently ancient stone bridge that carried the park's main walk across the stream, the favoured spot was well hidden by trees, and the only access a tiny and overgrown footpath. Once I had penetrated the copse, however, I found a comfortably grassy bank and a stretch of cheerful, fast flowing water.

Settling myself down, I found I was completely hidden from every angle. I set up my rod and line, wedging them into position with rocks in order that the effort I might have to expend in tending them would be minimal: for, of course, not only did I have no clue what I was doing (and was, moreover, grateful that the gardener had not insisted on my taking a fly rod which would have exposed my ignorance yet further) but I had no real intention of trying to catch anything. I lay back on the soft grass, and opened my book.

With time, however, the sun rose higher in the sky and I grew hot. My wool tailcoat and waistcoat hung on me with increasing heaviness, my cravat constricted my neck, and I felt the sweat trickle down my back. I began to debate with myself the propriety of removing my outer garments. Who was likely to see me? None of the ladies, surely, would venture here for fear of tearing their dresses on the brambles at the entrance. At worst I might encounter my host, or one of the menservants, none of whom would be discomposed by the sight of a gentleman in a state of *déshabillé*. Accordingly I removed the offending articles, and clad only in shirt and breeches, returned to the perusal of my book.

The day grew warmer, and the book—despite having been the most interesting-looking volume I had managed to find in the library—was dull. Despite myself, my eyes began to close, and the book to fall from my grasp.

It was the sound of voices that returned me to abrupt consciousness. I panicked, clutching my clothes towards me—until common sense reminded me that I could not be seen.

The voice came closer. I could hear several women's voices, Sophia's among them, and also the deeper tones of Captain Wainwright, from which I deduced that the morning's sport must have ended. A sudden sharpness to the sound of their footsteps indicated that they had gained the bridge. Once there, however, the party paused, and engaged themselves in looking for fish.

The scream—Sophia's scream, a cry of genuine terror—ripped through the bucolic peace of the park like the report of scandal through a ballroom. It was accompanied by the rasp of stone against stone, and followed by a heavy splash and the upraised voices of the whole company. Wainwright's voice was audible above the rest. 'Sophia!' he cried. 'My God! Sophia!'

You must remember that I had but a moment to make my decision, and I was still half asleep. Should I rescue her? She was in no real danger: should I not leave it to Wainwright to perform this gentlemanly office? And yet—and yet—Wainwright's posthuman adaptations were for salt water! Submersion in fresh water would not harm him in the City, but the effects of osmosis, I knew, would transmute his healthy green skin to an ugly purple for the several hours it would take for the balance of his body fluids to be restored. How could I condemn my friend to such indignity?

I plunged myself into the waters of the stream and, half staggering, half swimming, struck out with all speed in the direction of the bridge.

'Have no fear, Miss Sophia!' I cried. 'I will save you!'

Gasping and spluttering I gained the bridge, and half-blinded with water began to cast around for the young lady I was intent on rescuing. The only obstruction I encountered, however, was a weighty section of parapet that had apparently broken off and fallen into the water, the undoubted cause of the splash I had heard. Raising my eyes to the bridge itself I was able to see the damaged section from which it originated, and the assembled company cowering away from the broken edge and looking down at me, as I stood there in my dripping shirtsleeves, with undisguised amazement. Wainwright, I saw, had pulled Sophia protectively towards him, but this, it seemed, was not to the taste of the young lady, who appeared to be resisting the embrace.

The assembled company surveyed me in my wet undershirt in appalled silence. As for me, I was too embarrassed to move, let alone speak: but not too embarrassed to see what else was happening. For approaching the bridge from all directions, alerted no doubt by Sophia's screams, was a whole host of servants. There were far more than might ever be needed to mount even the most sophisticated of rescue operations, and of all stations: from boot boy to butler to governess. And each and every one bore that same expression of rapt hunger that I had previously marked on the visages of the footman and the scullion.

Sophia was the first to recover her composure. Fighting her way out of Captain Wainwright's embrace, she moved to a safe area of parapet, leaned over, and smiled. 'Such gallantry, Mr Davenport,' she cooed, 'I assure you it is most unnecessary.'

'I—I assure you, Miss Sophia, I thought only of your comfort.'

She gave a coy smile. 'It does not follow that your attentions are unwelcome, sir,' she replied.

I was to endure a number of such comments over the course of the next few hours, and this, united with the teasing of the rest of the company and the stony silence of Wainwright, would normally have mortified me. There was, however, something else occupying my mind, providing a welcome distraction. The strange behaviour of the servants had triggered something in my memory.

Unfortunately, the rest of the day was to provide me with no opportunity to follow up my suspicions. My hosts had arranged such a plethora of entertainments through afternoon and evening as allowed no leisure for investigation. It was not until the company had retired at last to bed that I was able to take a candle and make my way through the dark silence of the house to the library.

The volume was where I remembered it, and to my surprise it fell open naturally at the page I needed. I carried it and the candle over to the table, and settled down to peruse the article in its entirety.

'Whilst the behaviours of other parasitic species of the genus Homo may be more physically *damaging to the host, the need of the Ettin to be close to sources of strong emotion when feeding is often considered, at the very least, to be distasteful...'*

'Mr Davenport.'

The voice came out of the silent darkness, and I nearly jumped out of my seat. But I knew that tone of arch coyness.

'Good God, Miss Sophia! You must not be here, alone, at night! What if we were to be seen? Your reputation!'

She had come within the ambit of the candlelight, by now, and I could see her face. It was beautiful in the dim glow, but, at that moment, less endearing than ever. She wore a strange, half-smile. 'And if you were to destroy my reputation, Mr Davenport, then who should make amends but yourself?'

And then I understood. I stared in horror. 'You would choose marriage on such terms? On the basis of an entrapment?' I asked.

The smile remained, but grew hard. 'I would have marriage on *any* terms, Mr Davenport. I died at the age of nineteen, from a putrid fever, yet unwed—and here I remain in the City, still nineteen and still unmarried. My parents brought me here to Highbury within days of my resurrection, and I have never left it since. Can you imagine what it is like, to live here year after year, for *decades*, without variety of person or place? Can you comprehend?'

'Then leave!' I cried. 'What is there to make you stay? You have no need to ensnare me into matrimony to make good your escape!'

'Leave? Friendless and without protection or means of support?'

'This is the City! You make your own friends and your own support!'

'And this is your idea of chivalry, Mr Davenport? Where are your tender concerns for my reputation now?'

'Miss Sophia, do you have really no comprehension of just how little a reputation—at least, this kind of reputation—means, outside of Highbury? Do you not understand just how, how *artificial* all of this is?'

'Artificial. Yes, I understand that this is a common enough complaint against our society, from those who do not know how to value deportment and good breeding.'

'No! That's not what I mean at all! Here, listen to this,' and I began to read.

'Insofar as the origins of the Ettin are understood, the relevant period of their evolution took place on a planet inhabited by only one other edible animal species: a herbivorous and sentient life-form. The largely carnivorous Ettin made use of their weak telepathic abilities to aid them in the tracking of this species as their prey, sensing and homing in on strong sources of fear.

'Over millennia, the biological link between the telepathic detection of fear and the act of eating became more entrenched. As a result, it has ultimately become impossible for the individual Ettin to secrete the enzymes that it needs to digest its food, unless the relevant nerve centres of the creature's brain have been stimulated by the reception of appropriately acute telepathic signals from another sentient being. The stimulus need not be fear: any unpleasant emotion will do, including, but not limited to sadness, anger, and even at a pinch, extreme embarrassment.

'It has been argued that, within the context of the City, it would be unnecessary for the Ettin to seek out the stimulus of acute emotion given that the inability to digest food would not be of material harm to them in this environment. In practice, however, it seems that the Ettin are not only physically but also psychologically addicted to the vicarious experience of emotion...'

'This is all very educational, Mr Davenport, but it cannot have any relevance to *me*.'

'Do you not comprehend?'

'I confess, I do not.' Her voice was cold.

'Consider, Miss Sophia, the strange behaviour of your servants, the expressions on their faces, their habit of appearing out of thin air every time there is a demonstration of emotion! The distress of your scullery maid at being kept always below stairs, away from the family! Is it not obvious?'

'I am not in the habit of making a study of the reactions of servants.'

'Your servants, Miss Sophia, are Ettin.'

'Do not be so ridiculous.'

I lost my temper. 'Dammit, look at the *facts*, Sophy! You've got this, this *bizarre*, sterile, stagnant society, full of repressed emotion, and the servants are falling over each other to drink it all in! What better place for them to hide, to get their fixes, than here! They can't hunt any more, they can't frighten you with physical harm, but they can prey on *you* here, where there's a constant bedrock of raw emotion that's all the more potent for being so consistently suppressed! And you all just stand by and let it happen!'

'I do not recall giving you permission to use my name in this familiar way, Mr Davenport.'

'Think for a minute, think! Use your *brain*, for once. You've got a District bursting with unmarried people, *young* people by any consideration that makes sense, all full of feelings and hormones and God knows what, all bound by these ridiculous societal restrictions. But other than the elopements of servants—

of Ettin themselves—how many attachments ever come to fruition?'

'There is my sister and Mr Hill.' Sophia's voice was no longer just cold, it was icy.

'Who are not yet married, as Mr Hill has been called away on business to the Romuline, and nobody knows when he is to return.'

'And my cousin Fanny and Mr Farraday.'

'A match that has been forbidden by your uncle. And Miss Baird and the Reverend Hugh Lanning wait upon his gaining the living of Barton, even though that is dependent on the death of the present incumbent, which can never be, and Miss Henrietta Saunders and Lieutenant Barron wait upon his being offered a command! Has there been any marriage here, here in Highbury, within memory?'

'I—I do not recall.'

'And there's Miss Green and Mr William Lee who are considered by her mother to be too young to marry, despite the fact that both of them are more than 100 years old, and the curate who calls on your family far more often than the calls of pastoral duty could possibly demand and your youngest brother who gazes in his turn across the church at the curate like a lovesick sheep! And nobody ever thinks to get out! You have all been brainwashed! Your society is being *engineered*, Sophy, engineered by a race who have a vested interest in maintaining this continuous festering mess of suppressed desperation!'

In my excitement, I had not realised that my voice had risen. I was brought back violently to myself by the sound of a throat being cleared in the darkness behind me.

'Mr Davenport, Lady Horatia's compliments, and she would be grateful if you would do her the honour of waiting upon her at Warrington Hall at your earliest convenience.'

I turned around. It was the footman. 'For God's sake, man, it's the middle of the night!' I cried, the more sharply for the shock I had suffered.

'I fear her ladyship will brook no refusal.'

'I am engaged at present with Miss Sophia.'

But Sophia had turned her face away from me. 'This interview is at an end. I must beg you to importune me no longer,' she said, and swept from the room.

I turned to the footman. 'Please convey my respects to Lady Horatia, and tell her I will wait upon her first thing in the morning.'

'I'm afraid that will not do, sir.'

'What do you mean, will not do?'

A slight scuffling, followed by a glimmer of light, drew my attention to the door. Another figure, this one carrying a lantern, came into to the room, followed by another, and then yet another.

'You would be wise to do as Lady Horatia suggests, sir,' said one of the figures.

I looked from one face to another, illuminated in the dim light, and recognised them as the male servants of the house, and I began to feel afraid.

In the end, it was easier to go with the servants than to resist. They might not have been able to hurt me, but they could certainly have dragged me before her ladyship by force, and I wished to avoid the indignity. The only person we encountered as we left the house was Bessie, once again carrying coal scuttle and brush, who squeaked and flattened herself against the wall as we passed.

Despite the lateness of the hour, I was brought before Lady Horatia in her drawing room, where she received me, fully dressed, and with as much decorum and ease as if I were making a commonplace morning call.

'If you must conduct conversations after the Maitland family has retired, Mr Davenport, you would do as well to lower your voice. James,' Lady Horatia nodded in the direction of the footman, 'could hear you all the way from the servants' hall where he was assisting the butler with the silver.'

'I fail to see why my nocturnal activities should merit my being dragged through the countryside in the middle of the night to see *you,'* I replied. 'If Mr Maitland were inclined to take offence at my late-night use of his library, surely he could tell me so himself.'

'It is not the use of the library *per se* that concerns me,' she replied. 'But rather the nature of the deductions you made whilst so doing.'

'About the Ettin.'

'Indeed.'

'So you know about that.'

'There is little that goes on in Highbury I do *not* know about, Mr Davenport.'

'Then why—I mean, surely—with your connections—you could *do* something about it!'

'And why would I want to do *that*, Mr Davenport?'

I was lost for words. But Lady Horatia had not finished. She smiled sweetly at me, and continued in a reflective voice.

'The thing about the Ettin, Mr Davenport—well, as you have read, the Ettin are *drawn* to emotion. Many live in Highbury, as you have deduced. You might even say it is an ideal habitat for them. But it is by no means the only place where they can thrive. Where else might an Ettin be assured of reliable sources of suppressed fear and rage: where might they find a guaranteed diet of betrayal, ambition and the clash of rampant egos?'

'I don't follow.'

'Politics, Mr Davenport, politics! The Ettin infiltrate every conceivable layer of politics, from the very lowest to the Council House itself!'

'How is this not common knowledge?'

'It is not in the nature of the Ettin to draw attention to themselves. Besides, they have no political agenda as a group: it is rare for them to join forces over any given issue and thus risk revealing themselves. There is only one exception to this rule of behaviour... one issue concerning which the Ettin will rally. Perhaps you can guess what it is?'

I thought. 'Highbury?' I hazarded.

'Well *done*, Mr Davenport!' She smiled at me as if I were a favourite child who had recited a difficult lesson.

'Are *you* an Ettin?'

Lady Horatia laughed, a high, tinkling laugh, seemingly of genuine amusement. '*Me*? Goodness no, Mr Davenport. But perhaps you begin to understand. The Ettin are inclined to be grateful, you see. And someone who is prepared to, perhaps, keep a maternal watch over a place that the Ettin hold dear, someone who will work to maintain the status quo, to maintain the excesses of emotion that make this place so attractive, to have a word in the ear of a papa here, to send a young man away to sea there, to make sure the young people of the place are brought up, shall we say, with the right attitudes and the correct behaviours... Well, Mr Davenport, such a person might find themselves in receipt of a great deal of gratitude. Gratitude, moreover, from a group of people who, whilst self-effacing, are perfectly placed to advance the interests of those they consider their friends.'

'In other words, you're in this for your political career.'

Lady Horatia smiled. 'Your speed of apprehension does you credit, Mr Davenport.'

'So where does this leave me? What happens now? I assume, given the way that Mr Maitland's copy of Dr Clutterbuck's book falls open so readily at the page on which the Ettin are described, that I am not the first person to have made these deductions. And yet these things have yet to be made public.'

'Well you might ask, Mr Davenport. Look around you.'

I looked around at the assembled servants. Each one wore the intense expression that I had come to know and understand—indeed, James looked to be on the brink of physical climax. It was unsurprising that they should: despite the bravado of my words, I was truly terrified.

'The understanding of most people concerning the Ettin,' said Lady Horatia, 'is that while distasteful, their proclivities are not actually harmful to their prey unless followed up by the actual infliction of physical harm that is, of course, impossible in the City. I regret for your sake, Mr Davenport, that this is not, in fact, the case.'

I was beyond false bravado now. 'What then?' I croaked.

'Have you heard of "positive feedback", Mr Davenport?'

'Of course.'

'When an Ettin telepathically detects fear in another organism, certain pleasure centres of its brain are stimulated—which, in turn, initiates a whole host of reactions, including, as you well know, the release of certain hormones. Some of these hormones further stimulate the telepathic pathways of the creature's brain, leading them to not only receive a telepathic signal, but also to emit one. To the brains of the Ettin, this is harmless, but in the underdeveloped telepathic neural pathways of the average human basic the telepathic signal can have the effect of actually *increasing* the fear felt by the other organism. This increased fear is, in turn, detected by the Ettin.' She paused, and smiled. 'Do you understand why I am explaining this to you?'

I raised my head. Her implication was only too clear. 'You want to make me more afraid,' I said.

'Correct, Mr Davenport! As you have no doubt already comprehended, this is not an effect that is likely to occur during normal Ettin and human-basic interactions. The race could hardly maintain their secret status if it were so. But in a situation like this, where we have a man who is very, very afraid—and I trust you are *very* afraid, Mr Davenport—and where there are many Ettin present in very close physical proximity, then the effects of the positive feedback loop on the human basic brain can be quite emotionally crippling. Crippling to the extent that you will be left a babbling fool for the remainder of your *very* long life, and nobody will ever again take seriously a word you say. If you wish to run, Mr Davenport, now would be the time to do so.'

The odds were hopeless enough, as she well knew, but of course, I had to try. Like the hunted prey I had quite literally become, I raised my head and my eyes darted from side to side in search of escape.

Perhaps with the idea of prolonging their sport, the Ettin had left the route to the door relatively clear. I feinted, darting towards it, then abruptly changed my course, and ran with all possible speed for the window.

They allowed me almost to touch the sill. Indeed, the brief burst of hope generated by the possibility of escape seemingly so near, and the subsequent quashing of that hope as they laid hands upon me caused such transports of ecstasy among my captors that more than one groaned aloud. I fought with everything I possessed: but it was not enough. With humiliating speed they wrestled me to the ground and before many more moments had passed they had me pinned there, spreadeagled: immobile, utterly terrified and surrounded at close quarters by faces whose ecstatic rigidity made them look (even by City standards) barely human.

'Is this how you demonstrate your hospitality to *all* your guests, Lady Horatia?'

The interjection came from the direction of the door. I could not see who was speaking, but I knew the voice well enough. 'Sophia!' I gasped.

Lady Horatia was similarly bewildered. 'What are *you* doing here?' she cried.

'I intend to rescue Mr Davenport.'

'And how, pray, do you plan to effect this?' replied her ladyship, recovering her poise.

'You would not wish the events of this night to be made public, I think,' replied Sophia. She sounded extraordinarily calm, in marked contrast to my own emotions. It may or may not have been my imagination, but I could *feel* the influence of the malign telepathic waves around me, penetrating my skull, filling my head...

'You foolish child! What do you think would prevent me from dealing with you as I am dealing with Mr Davenport?'

'Do you really think my father would stand for that?' replied Sophia. I thought I could make out her figure, now, illuminated by the soft glow of the candles, but it was a dim, nebulous shape which seemed to grow even more insubstantial as the uncanny sensation of pressure inside my head grew ever stronger.

'Your father would never *know*, child.'

'Please be good enough not to trifle with me, Lady Horatia. It took but a few moments' reflection, once I had recovered from the shock of Mr Davenport's revelations about our servants, to realise that such wholesale exploitation of the population of Highbury could hardly be carried out without the knowing complicity of at least *some* of the more prominent residents. My father may wink at what is taking place here, he may choose to ignore the more subtle forms of duress under which his kin is placed in return for the stability of family life he so covets, but I am quite certain he would not countenance the emotional mutilation of one of his daughters. I am also quite certain it would not take him long to deduce who was to blame for such mutilation. And your position of influence in Highbury may be secure, Lady Horatia, but not so secure that it could long withstand the opposition of my father, were he to choose to broadcast your actions abroad.'

Lady Horatia was taken aback, I could see. She rallied, however. 'And what solution would you suggest?' she replied, with a tolerable resumption of her former assurance.

'Let Mr Davenport go, let him leave Highbury. He has no influence in the wider City, he cannot harm you. And were he to try, you have my continued presence here as guarantee of his good behaviour. You would not wish harm to come to me on your account, would you sir?'

I shook my head fervently.

It was a barely perceptible flick of Lady Horatia's fingers, but the Ettin saw, and understood. At once they released their multiple holds on me and began to withdraw, the pressure inside my skull decreasing even as they did so.

Lady Horatia looked at me. 'You understand, Mr Davenport, that my contacts are widespread, very widespread indeed. I will be watching you. There is *nowhere* in the City that is outside the influence of the Ettin. I am prepared to risk, for the sake of the good opinion of my neighbours, letting you go tonight: but should I hear that you have broken our agreement, neither you or Miss Maitland will be safe. Do you understand?'

'I do. I most certainly do.'

'Mr Davenport, you are free to go,' she said. 'You may thank Miss Maitland for your good fortune.'

'I will escort Mr Davenport back to my father's house,' said Sophia. She looked at me. 'I believe that under the circumstances we may overlook the impropriety.'

Sophia swept from the house in silence, with me at her heels. Once, however, she was out of sight and earshot of the hall she faltered, staggered, seemed almost about to faint. 'I was by no means certain of that stratagem meeting with success,' she said, her voice tremulous.

'How did you know where I was?' I asked.

'After I'd had time to think, I went back to look for you in the library, and Bessie told me where you'd been taken. She seems to feel sympathetic towards you.'

I looked into Sophia's eyes. She was not the girl I had thought her to be. To have weathered the shock of all her preconceptions and prejudices about her place of residence being overturned; to have deduced her father's involvement and to have used this understanding to come up with a plan of rescue so quickly; to be so brave, so quick witted, so poised in the face of danger! Sophia, with all her affectedness of manner, her desperate flirting, her wilfulness: all these things were nothing more than the manifestations of a lively intellect and a strong and active mind desperate for stimulation!

I now suddenly comprehended that she was exactly the woman who, in temperament and intellect, would most suit me. Wainwright's desires be damned: her understanding and character, though dissimilar to my own, would answer all my wishes for my afterlife. Dearest, loveliest, most courageous of women!

I fell to my knees. 'Miss Maitland. You must grant me the opportunity to tell you how fervently I esteem and adore you. Would you do me the honour of consenting to be my wife?'

She smiled at me, but it was a sad smile. 'I thank you for the honour of your proposal sir, but it is not within my power to accept.'

I could not answer. I knelt there, my jaw hanging open, silenced.

'Do not dally, sir. We must return to the house before daybreak.'

I struggled to my feet. 'May I—may I demand to know the reason why I am thus refused? I understood you to be desirous of—to be expecting my addresses.'

'We can hardly hope our marriage would ever take place in Highbury.'

'Sophy! There is a whole wide City out there! We can do whatever we like, go wherever we like!'

'But then I would have to leave here.'

'You wish to *stay*? After everything that has occurred? After all you have learned?'

'If I do not stay, Mr Davenport, I cannot hope to change things.'

'Change things? Lady Horatia will hardly consent to *that*.'

She swung around to face me. Her eyes shone in the darkness with the zeal of the visionary. 'Mr Davenport. Up until this point, the whole—from birth to death to resurrection until now—the *whole* of my life has been spent in idleness and ennui. Now, however, I understand—I finally *know* what my afterlife's work is to be. I will stay, I will maintain the outward appearance of docility and good breeding, but I will *change* things. I may have to work slowly, with subtlety and discretion, but I will no longer suffer my family and friends to labour under this yoke of oppression without opposition.'

'Then allow me to remain with you, to help you!'

'Lady Horatia will not countenance *that*, either. You must leave Highbury, for your own safety.'

'Then what shall I *do*?'

'Go, Mr Davenport. Live your afterlife. Be happy.'

'Sophy—'

'Yes?'

'This state of affairs cannot last forever, Sophy. Some day—some day, Lady Horatia will no longer be in power, and things *will* change. Might I—do I ask too much—to *hope*? To believe that one day we might be together?'

She smiled at me. ‘Perhaps,’ she said.

And with that, my Sophy, beautiful, brave, noble Sophy, turned from me and walked away into the darkness.

ABOUT A GIRL

Dale Smith

They called themselves The Twenty-Seven. My brother said he'd used to listen to Nat Jaffe as a kid, but I didn't know him. I didn't know anything from back then. I've only ever known the City. Even my family I had to get to know here. I remember my brother introducing me to my mother, the shiver of revulsion as she reached through me looking for something human. I was born in the city, despite what anybody would say.

They called themselves The Twenty-Seven, and nobody cared – could anybody say they hadn't lived a long life, after 250 years in the City? – but perhaps that was why I went to see them. It was mostly people from the Anubian District, each as out of place as me I suppose. But he'd seen me there dancing, hadn't dared come over himself of course. He'd sent Kristen instead.

'Hey. You wanna meet Kurt?'

And that had been that.

'You want to see something?' Kurt asked.

This was the third night I'd come to watch The Twenty-Seven, and the third that Kristen had brought me backstage. She was over at the back of the room now, drinking rum with Amy while they fought their way through *Me and Mrs Jones*. I'd thought they were sisters at first – they had the same long dark hair and tired eyes, and bickered in that gentle way that other people's families seemed to. But when they spoke, they sounded nothing alike: Kurt had to tell me that Amy's accent was British, and laughed when I told him I'd given up trying to remember ancient geography.

'I made it,' Kurt said, holding out a battered cardboard box.

Inside was a doll, a work of art perhaps. It had the head of a baby, some kind of toy with one shattered glass blue eye, but its limbs were metal claws pinned to the body with twists of wire. The bottom half of the body had been sawn completely off, leaving the doll hollow inside all the way up to her skull.

'It's beautiful,' I said, running a bothrium down a rough edge of solder.

Kurt smiled like I'd passed some kind of test.

'Is it supposed to be me?'

He picked up a cigarette from the table and lit it, holding out the pack to me. Most people don't do that. They don't trust that I can be just as dexterous with my bothria as they can. Or more likely they just didn't like seeing a six-week-old baby smoking. But Kurt didn't check himself at all. That was one of the most beautiful things about him: that he had such a posthuman attitude for someone of his age. I think I was already a little in love with him.

'I made them when I was a kid,' he said, giving every indication of not really watching me at all. 'I've been making them here for a while too. I guess there's so much time, you're going to do everything again one day. You can keep it if you want to. I mean I don't mind.'

'Thank you!' I said.

I think I smiled at him a little too long, but he smiled back and there we were alone with each other, just for a moment. There's something addictive in moments like that. Something chemical that is one time only and never comes back quite the same. People fall in love in moments like that, and miss them a little even if they stay with that person for the rest of their lives. Except of course when the rest of your life is forever, every itch gets a little harder to ignore. I'm not saying every married couple in the City has broken up, but enough have in the last 250 years to make you wonder if everything is just a matter of time.

There was a crash as Amy wobbled a little too far trying to make for the rest room. I could hear her giggling at the bottom of the staircase: she must have flipped clean over the railing and down onto the street outside. Kurt rolled his eyes, but he still passed over another bottle of brandy when Amy reappeared, her beehive bent at an alarming angle and a look of mock disgust on the face below it. There appeared a sheepish little wild-haired grandfather behind her, and before he could say anything Amy had grabbed him and planted a kiss on every cheek.

'You want to go some place else?' Kurt asked.

I did, of course.

'So you're the same age as my grandma,' Kurt had that look. So serious that he could only be kidding. 'You know that's pretty wrong, yeah?'

I flicked at him with the tip of a bothrium.

'I'm 250,' I answered innocently. 'Same as you.'

He didn't smile, just looked nervously out of the cab window. It was raining outside, but that was nothing new. Everything here was rain smeared blue and neon orange, and gigantic geisha faces smiled demurely down at us from video advertisements on the buildings. The air was greased with smoke, since every second person seemed to have a cigarette in their mouth. Kurt was tapping his fingers against the window of the cab, but that might not be nerves. I knew there was always some song nagging at him, and he only ever seemed to properly relax when he had a guitar on his lap.

'Is it far?' he asked, giving in and lighting a cigarette.

'Two minutes,' the driver called back.

Kurt closed his eyes. The cigarette in his mouth trembled in time with his heartbeat.

'You've really never left Mappamundi before?' I asked.

'Seattle,' Kurt corrected automatically.

He took another pull at his cigarette, and I could tell he was trying to think of the most nonchalant comeback he could. There was something endearing in its childishness, like having boys fight over you, but there was something sad in it too. He couldn't risk having anyone dismiss him. Every experience, every opinion had to be eased into conversation so that it could be disowned if it wasn't accepted. It was so sad to see the quiet confidence that surrounded him on stage evaporate the moment he stepped out of the spotlight.

'I used to tour a lot,' he said eventually, as if that explained it.

I let two bothria fall softly on his lap.

'It will be alright,' I told him softly. 'He'll like you. And if he doesn't, we're not that close. It doesn't matter.'

'You're not that close?' Kurt snorted. 'You and your *twin* brother?'

'I died when we were six weeks old,' I said with a shrug. 'The twin he built up in his head was never me, and I never knew him at all. I don't think of him like that.'

'So I should worry when you take me to meet Akroates then?'

I gave an involuntary click of my tongue.

'I don't think of him like that either.'

Kurt seemed to relax a little at that, and looked at me properly for the first time since we'd got in the boxy yellow taxi. I gave him a smile, and he turned away to hide the grin that broke out across his face. I caressed a bothrium around his jaw, and then quickly flicked the cigarette from his mouth and back into my own with a grin. I could see the taxi driver scowl at us in his rear-view mirror, but I had become adept at ignoring that. I was a grown woman, and I wasn't going to pretend otherwise for jerks like him.

'You really don't remember anything about being alive?'

'Alive is now,' I looked out of the window. Japanese food and greatcoats as far as the eye could see. 'What I would've had if I hadn't have died wouldn't have been anything I'd call living.'

'But you don't remember?' he pressed. 'Nothing?'

'Memory is all about context.' I said, but I had to look somewhere else while I lied to him. 'I didn't have the experience to process what was happening to me. My brain wasn't fully developed. How much do you remember about being born?'

It wasn't a complete lie. On Resurrection Day, I was just a six-week old baby like any other: somebody had to look after me, and Akroates was the one. He was the one who stayed with me in the deme house, even as the others found their families or their way and drifted off. He arranged for the health visitors, a posthuman family unit from Century Azure, and made sure I wasn't hungry while they looked for my genetic next of kin.

Around the time that the family started to realise the City would only need healthcare for a finite period, it became pretty obvious that whilst I was getting smarter, I wasn't getting older. Apparently it happens to some of the infant mortalities: most of them are just like any other City-born and grow to maturity before they stop ageing, but some of us just never do. So far, nobody's managed to work out why, but given how comfortable I feel in my own skin, I like to think that deep down somewhere we just make a choice. One of the last things the family did was bond me to my exo-bothria so that it could get to know me. That was how I not only took my first steps at the age of seven months, but I took them across the ceiling of the hospital ward. Then they applied the nano-stems, and then they disappeared from the City completely. Some of the posthuman societies are as rigidly compartmentalised as Feudal Japan: with their function redundant, I don't know if the family would have had the ability to adapt, even if it had occurred to them. I sometimes wonder where they went: I know they are still alive, but what kind of life it is...

But whatever happened to them, they gave me the stems, which are why I can eat anything other than milk and see in full colour. No-one really knows if they're also why a mind that is physically that of a six week old baby can function like a cold cloud-cognate, but they are certainly responsible for my memory. They went through my synapses like a good secretary with a few hours to kill, and now everything I've ever done – every thought I've ever had – is neatly cross-referenced and ready to recall with barely a millisecond lag.

I remember everything. I can choose to forget, if I really want to, but even then the backups are readily available. Of all the things that I've become since my short, sad original life, that is the one I've found hardest to come to terms with.

'This is it,' the taxi driver spat as we pulled up outside the restaurant.

Kurt looked out the window, and made no effort to move.

'Look on the bright side,' I told him. 'It's not like he can have you killed.'

The restaurant was filled with people in evening wear sitting down to plates of sushi like it was the most inexplicably alien thing the City had ever shown them. That was the problem with the theme districts as far as I was concerned – the City had opened all of humanity up to the strange wonders of life in every age of its existence, but these odd little suburbs only ever told you about the imagination of one person in one time. But whenever my brother decided to summon me, it was always to this one place. He would give you a hundred different interpretations of his motives, but part of me suspects that it's simply ego.

He was sitting at the back of the restaurant, that familiar round grey flecked figure trying very hard to sink into the background. He looked up as we came in, but didn't give any indication. He wouldn't want to draw attention to himself. Kurt saw him too, and I felt him tense beside me.

'Don't worry,' I whispered, and we walked across the room together.

'Hello, Jane,' he said softly. He motioned for Kurt to take a seat, and I perched myself on one end of the table. 'Thanks for coming.'

It was only once you got close to him, and only if you knew where to look, that you saw the people satelliting him so carefully. There was a young man at the table next to us, a posthuman with bioluminescent filaments waving softly in the breeze, a woman who was wider than she was tall with a face like a hatchet. He managed to look slightly embarrassed by them, realising the absurdity of having protection in the City, but I knew from experience that he wasn't above appealing to them when he found a particular conversation troubling.

'Hi Phil,' I said. 'How're you doing?'

'And you must be Kurt,' he said, smiling politely up and holding out a hand. 'I've heard your music. It's very good. It made me wonder whether you were directly referencing the Dharmakaya Buddha?'

Kurt didn't move.

'I guess,' he said.

Phil looked slightly awkwardly at his hand for a few moments, and then let it drop back into his lap. Kurt just continued to gaze at him with undisguised boredom – he had obviously decided that my brother was not somebody that he needed to impress. Once he decided that about you, you might as well not exist. In Phil's case, he was probably right: there was some crossover between the circles that Kurt moved in and Phil's, but that crossover was me and I had never yet changed my opinions of somebody to keep my brother happy.

'Can I get you lunch?' Phil said, looking around as if he had only just realised we were in a restaurant.

'So somebody told me you were big in France once,' Kurt drawled from nowhere. 'I mean, I've never heard of you, but somebody said you were big. In France.'

Phil turned back around very slowly.

'Jerry Lewis was big in France,' Kurt continued. He paused for a moment. 'Of course, he was big in the States too.'

Phil looked at me with a raised eyebrow. For a moment, he looked as if he expected me to leap to his defence. No matter who else he had become, Phil still wasn't the sort of person who would stand up for himself. He's just spend the next week thinking of all the possible ways he *should* have defended himself, and map each of their varied consequences in intricate detail.

But of course, he had other people to stand up for him now.

A man on a nearby table stood up meaningfully.

'It's alright,' Phil said, waving a hand. The man sat down again, and Phil turned to me. 'I know you think... well, we don't have to go over what you think of me again. But how much do you know about this guy? My best working theory still has you as genuinely my sister. I'm worried about you.'

'Phil, you worry about the intrinsic nature of reality,' I said. 'I don't think that leaves much time for anything else.'

'Do you know how he died?' Phil insisted.

'As I understand it, the best working theory is that a great philosopher saw a glimpse of VALIS and destroyed that false reality for everyone.'

'So now you're mocking me again?' Phil turned indignant. As his voice started to rise, heads started to turn towards us. 'Because I don't want to see my sister spend the rest of her time here with a married, suicidal junky?'

I didn't look at Kurt, but I could feel him sneer beside me. My bothria flicked in irritation, something so instinctive I couldn't stop them from upsetting a cup on the adjourning table. One of Phil's bodyguards leapt up immediately and started making placatory noises at the woman wearing a snakeskin bra and the dregs of a synthetic coffee.

'Narcotics?' I hissed. '*You're* going to lecture me on narcotics?'

'Jane, calm down!'

A small crowd was starting to knot around us, blocking the narrow restaurant almost completely. But that made no difference to me: I just reached up with my bothria and clung to the ceiling, pulling myself up and scuttling upside down to the exit without another word. Kurt would have to make his own way out, and God alone knew what Phil would say to him without me there, but right then I didn't care.

Everything in life is just for a while, even in the City... so why did I feel forever trapped with my family's prehistoric attitudes?

'See now that's why people get freaked by you,' Kurt said softly. 'We're stuck with the same old skinny-ass bodies that drove us crazy before, forever. But you spider-babies, you get to do cool shit like that. It's not fair, you know?'

Despite growing up in the City, despite 250 years of posthuman attitudes and influences, there's something in it that must be biological. I've never seen a posthuman angry, never seen them spit and bubble with the frustration of other people. Despite everything I am and try to be, there's still some part of me that is just another ordinary girl from 1920s Earth. But even still, I wasn't so human and blinkered that I couldn't see Kurt was trying to redirect us into a fight that wouldn't affect him whichever way it went.

'Which is the one you don't want me asking about?' I asked him.

Kurt just looked sullenly at the ground.

'You didn't tell me,' I know I was snipping at him, but as I say – some of it must be biological. 'You were worried about how I'd react to something that happened to you before Resurrection Day, for some reason. I just wondered which it was: the wife, the drugs or the suicide?'

Just for a moment, he looked like he might try to hit me.

'I thought you already knew!' he yelled.

'Oh Kurt,' I said, letting each honey-soaked word drip gently onto him. 'All of humanity lives here now. You're just not that famous.'

I didn't see Kurt for a few days after that.

I didn't see my brother, either: he obviously thought he had discharged his familial responsibilities enough by allowing for the possibility that I was genuinely his sister. If I'm honest, I was glad that I didn't see him. Our bond was doubly tenuous – back in a place that doesn't matter any more, the two of us didn't know each other – and he is just one of a breed of City people I find it hard to cope with. This place is heaven by any definition, but they deny it and distrust it and all for the same reason at the end of the day: they just aren't ready to let go of their old lives. It would be sad, if they weren't spoiling it for the rest of us.

I should have tried to see Kurt. But I didn't.

And then one night there was a knock at the door. I thought it might be Akroates – it wouldn't be the first time my brother had tried to appeal to me through him – but instead there was a little man with a shock of white hair and a bulbous nose.

'We haven't met,' he said. He looked nervous, but some people did around me. 'My name is Al. I...'

'You were backstage with the Twenty-Seven,' I said, not giving way to let him through. 'Three times. I have an exceptional memory.'

Al gave a little bow, looked back over his shoulder.

'I know Kurt,' he explained. His voice was soft, accented and grandfatherly. 'I believe that you and he are friends? I believe he needs a friend now.'

'Then he has you.'

The old man looked sheepish.

'I believe he needs a better friend than I have ever been,' he said, then took a step back. It looked for a moment like he might drop to his knees, but instead he held out a hand to me. 'Please. Come with me. If you want, you can always leave again.'

I hesitated. Even in the City, I hesitated.

But what choice did I really have?

Al led me into a part of Mappamundi I hadn't been into before, where most of the inhabitants seemed to be in various stages of cybernetic enhancement. The streets were kept in almost pitch darkness, since everybody walking down them could see in the dark. The buildings were dotted with silver domes that seemed to grow on the dusty brick like boils. Somehow they still felt run down: even without the cultural references, I could tell that this was a part of the City you didn't venture into after dark. Al pulled on a pair of infra-red *pince-nez* and gestured for me to follow him deeper in.

Soon we were in a room filled with little knots of people, also-people and post-people. Each was dressed according to their culture, but even the ones with barely any clothes at all appeared shabby and grey. There seemed to be no logic behind who was where, as if somebody had filled the space with all of humanity and then shaken it to see where they fell. Nobody looked up as Al pushed his way through, not even as I skittered over the uneven floor behind him. Some were deep in muttered conversation. Most were smoking something, glassy-eyed.

'This can't be right,' I told myself.

Al stopped and looked back at me strangely.

'You've never...?' he stopped, and his eyes widened. 'Your relationship with Kurt. It can't be... sexual?'

My bothria flicked dangerously.

'I don't see that being any of your concern,' I hissed.

He blinked silently for a moment, shaking his head only the tiniest amount.

'Of course, I –' his manners made him stammer, but then he broke off as his face contorted with disgust. 'No. No, I'm sorry. This is too much. I was mistaken in bringing you here. Go. Just go. Now.'

And he tried to push past me and disappear back into the grey crowds. But he was right: this was too much. Anger flared and my skin – my human skin – trembled. I caught him with a bothrium flicked around his waist, pulling him back to face me. He snarled and closed his eyes tight, unable to even look me in the face.

'I am an intelligent human being,' I spat at him, my bothria whirling in a blind rage. 'Why do you have to bring your primitive preconceptions here? This place is heaven – why must you troglodytes insist on trying to drag it back into hell?'

He froze, for a second, a millisecond, an age.

'Heaven?' he echoed softly.

His eyes were soft and brown, and they must have sparkled once in his life.

'Heaven?' he said again. It was all he could say for a moment. 'Look around you, madam. Does this look like heaven? Do you think these people think anything of the kind? This is hell, and we are in it.'

'If it is, then it's only because you insist on making it.'

'Me?' he laughed hollowly. 'I had no part in the making of this place. I have no beginning of a concept for a place such as this. I was a scientist – even when I was supposed to be something else, I was only ever a scientist. I would see some hint of how the universe worked, and I would nag it day and night until I had the best possible answer. And now I'm here. This City is so far beyond anything I could imagine, I can't even begin to phrase the question. My understanding of the universe was as a caveman's, throwing ash on the wood and praying to the gods to bring the fire back. And yet it was the only thing that meant anything to me. The City took it from me, and chains me here day by day to make sure I never forget.'

For a moment, I felt an overwhelming urge to have my brother near me. I looked around at the grey huddled shapes all about. No, this couldn't be right.

Al sneered at me and stood aside.

'There,' he spat. 'Take him.'

Lying face down on the ground was Kurt.

I carried him home like an ant taking its dinner back to the nest, lifted gently over my head as I scurried along. He didn't move, barely breathed, for the next two days. I have no idea what the drugs he had taken were, but despite everything I thought he might die. It was a strange feeling, not wanting him to leave but still part of me wanting to see something I had never seen in my entire long life.

I couldn't trust the world around me any more. I moved gingerly through my own home, not certain even the ground beneath me would stay true and hold. This is the land of second chances and make-believe. And yet...

There was another world underneath this one, a colder, greyer world. I had always thought them stubborn, those who clung on to the lives they had left behind, who refused to live in every possible moment the City offered them. Stubborn but essentially harmless, still touched in their own way by the magic of this place. The chance to live again, to grow beyond anything they could have ever been anywhere else. But there was another world, and I had seen it, even briefly. Everything its inhabitants had ever held onto had been torn away from them and burned to ash. They couldn't live in this City any more than I could have done without my exo-bothria.

That was all that separated us – without this one small anachronism, I would be there in the grey with Al and Kurt.

I tried not to think about it, tried to focus on Kurt and his recovery. But I remembered my mother reaching out for me that first time. Looking for the baby she had lost all those years ago in the heart of this machine. That shiver of revulsion.

What if it hadn't been directed at me, but at a city that would make her cope with such things day after day after day?

'I... uh,' he said on the third day. 'Where did you find me?'

I wasn't ready for that conversation just yet.

'What were you doing?' I asked him. 'Why, Kurt?'

He rolled over sullenly, but he could still feel my eyes on him. When he spoke, it was begrudgingly, and without looking in my direction.

'It wasn't serious,' he muttered. 'It's not like it can hurt.'

'Are you still an addict?'

He looked at me. I saw something in his eyes that I hadn't seen before, and realised it was clarity, honesty. I wondered then what he really thought of me. Had there been something between us, or was I just another collection of doll parts for him to shape and bend on a whim?

'All I ever wanted to be was a rock star, you know?' he said. 'Cool, loved, messed up, all that. But that didn't work out, and I needed something so I could cope. That didn't work out either, so I joined The Twenty-Seven. And now I'm here. I can't be anything else but me, and I know that doesn't work out well. I still need something to cope. There's a lot to cope with here.'

Looking at him, I knew it was the truth. More than that, I knew he'd never told me before because I hadn't wanted to hear it. I hadn't wanted to see that other world, and now I had I still didn't. Because what if it wasn't another world? What if it was the real world, and I just couldn't bear to live in it?

'You want to die?'

He laughed, but I don't know if it was at the idea, or the absurdity of the question.

'There's someone you should talk to,' he told me.

He reminded me of my brother, there was no getting away from it. Not in the way he looked – he was old and thin with mad staring eyes, and a sombre black suit as if in mourning for his own mortality. Not in the way he spoke, either, which was slow and certain, as if every word he ever said had been carefully scripted years beforehand and memorised well. But the way his world circled around him, the way people listened to him and moved the scenes without him seeming to ask or even notice – that reminded me of Phil, in the early days when people first started to listen to him.

'My name,' he drawled languidly, 'is Edmund Ruffin. I don't suppose you have heard of me.'

'No,' I answered honestly.

'I was, I am, a great patriot,' he continued without hint of disappointment. Whatever connection he had to Kurt, it wasn't a shared need for notoriety. 'Have you heard of a place called the Confederacy?'

'I never really knew anywhere but the City.'

'He means America,' Kurt interjected. He turned to Ruffin with something like diffidence. It made me realise that I had never really seen him talk with anyone he actually respected. 'Jane was born in America, sir.'

'Whereabouts?' Ruffin asked quickly.

Kurt shrugged, and gave me a look that told me to keep quiet. He didn't need to – I had never thought to ask where I had originally been born.

'Well I am sure we are kinsfolk,' Ruffin laughed easily, but coldly. 'And I'm pleased to meet you, miss. I've been meeting with a lot of folks, just recently. Talking to them about my life. Would you like to hear what I've been saying?'

And I knew that I wouldn't. Kurt had brought me here to have Ruffin tell me about death, about the one thing that had been missing from my life. I knew I didn't really know anything about it. My resurrected, reorganised memory could retrieve the moment, but it meant nothing. Pain, and then the absence of pain... and then Lazarus holding me like a new-made father, nervously begging me not to cry. That was all I knew of death, and all I needed to know in the City.

What good would it do if I found in truth I needed more?

'I died in 1865,' Ruffin began, letting words come cautiously, waiting for me to object. 'Truth be told, I took my own life, but I'm not afraid to admit that. I gather the world had moved on more than a little by the time you two came into it, but I had my reasons for what I did, and I believed – and still do – that they were good ones. I was an old man when I died, and not a well one. I left the world because it wasn't the way I would have it be, but also to clear the way for my boy. You understand.'

'Mr Ruffin,' I said. 'I'm sure I don't.'

He smiled, but not in amusement.

'I fought in a war, miss,' he said, with more than a little pride. 'At its heart, it was about who should decide what was best for us. That is why the war was never lost: General Lee might have surrendered, but I wasn't having those damned Yankee sonsofbitches telling me who I should call brother. I was too ill to fight, but no God I ever prayed to would judge me for resisting the only way I could.'

With all the distractions that there are around my face, it's quite rare that anyone ever looks me in the eyes. But Ruffin did, and I felt Kurt tense behind me, a jealous child whose parent has shown just a modicum of attention to another.

'Humanity is not a state, not an inheritance,' he told me softly, as if trying to lull me to sleep. 'It is a journey, nothing more. A progression from the primitive through to the civilised man. They denied that, placing the primitive side by side with the man and telling us we were equals. That is what I believed then, and what I still believe now. Because that is the other thing about humanity: we are stubborn little cusses, and we don't change our mind for any man once we've set it how we like it. And that's why I had to die, do you understand?'

'Because you wouldn't change your mind?'

'Exactly, exactly,' he nodded at me as if I'd confirmed a sad truth he'd long suspected. 'I'd tried to set the world how it suited me. I was one of the civilised. But so had my father thought before me, and his father before him. So thought my son, but he was a good boy and minded his father. Do you think the multitude of cross-bred monsters that infest this place look at us and see the civilised, or the primitive?'

'I think they just want to help us,' I countered.

'They are good sons, and they mind their fathers,' he said. 'But some day it will come to war, mind me. This place is not how I would have it, and I am not alone in that. None of us are too ill to fight now. Can't you see? No son can mind his father forever. That is why God saw fit to move us aside when our time is done. No father should be forced to fight his son, no son his father. This place is hell, if it is anything.'

'This is heaven,' I said automatically. 'This is the land of make-believe.'

He looked away sadly.

'I'm pleased you think so, miss, I truly am,' he said. 'But I'm afraid to my mind it cannot be. Because we are all here, from the first man to the next to the last, and we are all equals in this place. And I don't see how we can all be right about how the world works. The best we can do is try to join our maker, and let him decide.'

He was no prophet, that much was clear. He was just a bitter old man who hadn't wanted to share his life with those he deemed inferior, and now refused to spend eternity the same way. He had Kurt convinced, but then it wasn't hard to convince Kurt that he was missing something because he couldn't die.

'Did you get it?' he asked as we left.

I couldn't look at him.

'Kurt,' I tried to tell him. 'Can't you see how easy it is? This place is just what we make it. We don't need anything we don't already have. You just have to let go.'

'No,' he snapped. 'You didn't hear him. We don't change. We can't change. All we can do is die.'

'So you'll always be just some angry sad child who doesn't want his father to leave?' I asked. 'Don't you want to be more than that?'

He didn't say anything then, and he didn't say anything later. I thought I wouldn't see him again, but I found myself going to his flat a few weeks later. I half thought I might just forget it all, let it go and be whatever he needed me to be. Even crave a mortality that was beyond us all, now. The door was answered by a dirty blonde-haired woman who had obviously just tumbled out of bed wearing nothing but a wedding ring and a heart-shaped box around her neck.

She sneered down at me.

'You're done, bitch,' she said, and slammed the door.

I wouldn't see him again, and I didn't think that either of us would mind.

The Uptime Gate is the exit from the City, the only one that anyone sensible believes in. Outside is the real world, where you can live, love, leave, die. And if you do, you end up back in the City again. Because everything in life is just for a while, except being a Citizen of the City. That is forever, whether you want it or not. Whether you are happy, or sad, or suicidal. I could leave, but I could never leave.

Yesterday, that thought caused me no trouble at all. Today, it itches a little, but can easily be ignored. This is, after all, the land of make-believe and second chances. But what about tomorrow? Is my relationship with the City, with life, just like any other relationship I have seen? Given enough time, will it pall and fade until ultimately I just wanted it to end?

I sit and look out at the Gate.

But there is nowhere to go.

BRUISES

Dave Hoskin

She started by licking the bruise off my face.

I could feel the soft urgency of her tongue as it slid around my eye, the heat of her breath, and as she bit down into my eyelid I remembered the merest flicker of what it was like to feel pain.

I almost came then and there.

A big part of it was the way she looked at me, of course. That panther-focus in her eyes, that incredible *need* for somebody like me. This girl barely even knew me, but she didn't give a shit about my name or what I did. All she cared about was that I had a black eye, and that was enough for her to virtually devour the side of my face as we both struggled to get our clothes off.

She felt me fumbling as one of my shirt buttons refused to cooperate. Still licking greedily at my eye, she simply tore the shirt apart and then ripped off the last tatters of her blouse for good measure. We stumbled into her bedroom and I was pushed backwards onto her bed. She stood over me, grinning with the electricity of the moment, and then she playfully poked her tongue out at me. My bruise had turned it black, and she laughed at the look on my face when I realised what had happened. Then she unhooked her skirt and let it fall to the floor.

Turned around.

Her body suddenly seemed very small to me, very fragile. Her skin was pale in the late afternoon light and beside her I could see dust motes twisting in the air. She was wearing green undies and nothing else, and just below the hem, right at the top of her thigh was a perfect round bruise.

She didn't look round at me. Just stood there, knowing what I was staring at.

Quietly, I got off the bed and knelt behind her. I put my hands upon her hips. I kissed the base of her spine and felt her move ever so slightly beneath my mouth.

My fingertips moved down the outside of her thighs, teasing, caressing. I kissed her on her hip and on her arse. Finally I reached the site of her bruise and watched my breath prickle the tiny little hairs on her skin.

I stuck out my tongue until the very tip of it touched the bruise. I could taste salt and black and blue. I licked all the way around it, slow and delicate, as if it were dangerous somehow. I felt her body tensing under my hands and then relaxing as I took my tongue away.

Then I buried my face in her bruise.

Licked her skin clean.

Felt her *shiver*.

My name's Lazarus. I've been living in Drausinus District for most of my life. It's a very small part of the City and only open to certain types of Citizen, but for some reason, despite the fact I walk the streets every day, I'd never seen the girl before.

I was crossing a small bridge. It was a nice day with a brisk little breeze blowing. She was standing in the middle of the bridge, leaning on the rail and looking down at the water. I don't really remember what she was wearing; I just remember the skirt. It was short and light, and the breeze was toying with it as I got closer. The ripple caught my eye, and as I passed I turned my head to look at her.

That's when the wind just happened to blow the hem of her skirt up for a full three seconds.

I don't know if she noticed, don't know if she cared.

She was wearing white undies, I remember that very distinctly. And right below the hem, right below her arse... I saw a perfect round bruise.

Something hot shot through me and I stumbled, trying to keep looking without being obvious. I glanced up to make sure she hadn't caught me, and in the time it took to do that, the wind dropped her skirt.

The moment evaporated.

I kept walking, but now the girl had straightened up and headed off in the opposite direction. I stopped, pretending to admire the view, but when she was almost out of sight, I started to follow her.

It only took ten minutes to reach her home, but for the entire time I couldn't stop thinking about the secret beneath her skirt. I wanted to know what it meant and how it got there. I wanted to know if she had any more. Occasionally I did look at the rest of her body – she was tiny, slim, short black hair – but it never took me long to refocus on the bruise. When she finally reached her dingy block and disappeared inside, I waited. I watched carefully for a light, trying to decide what to do next.

Ten storeys up, a light flicked on. I made a precise note of its location.

Then I called my station commander and told him I'd seen a bruiser.

'How did it look?'

'I only caught a glimpse of it.'

'Come on Laz, you can do better than that.'

'It was round. Dark. Almost black.'

'So it looked fresh?'

Freya pointed at the board on the wall. Thousands of bruise-images were ranked according to size and severity. She scrolled the board down so I could see the freshest examples running across the top row. I gingerly pointed one out, and she maximised the image.

'Oh Laz, you're not *serious*.' Freya's eyes were bright. 'And it looked convincing?'

'Expert. That's why I'm here. There's no way she could have done it to herself.'

'Imagine if it were real...' Freya gave a little sigh and then guided me over to a chair. She sat me down, picked up a pair of sunglasses from a tray covered in props and instruments, and got me to put them on. She made a note of how much of my face they covered up, and then removed them. 'Now close your eyes,' she said. 'This won't hurt a bit. '

I did as she said. I heard her select an instrument and then something cold pressed into my eyelid. I'd watched Freya do this to other undercover agents, but this was the first time I'd got a bruise myself. I could feel her tracing the shape, and then she began smudging the edges with her thumb. She didn't bother being gentle. After all, she didn't need to be.

'Don't do *too* good a job, Freya. If you give him the fucking Mona Lisa his cover story won't make any sense.' I didn't open my eyes, but I recognised Bartholomew's voice. He'd been on edge ever since I'd reported the bruise sighting and he never did like being in Freya's little workshop. He called it 'the necessary evil'.

'It's alright, Bart. I'll keep it down to Dogs Playing Poker just for you.'

'Are you going to teach him how to do that himself? I want him to know the basics.'

'So you want him totally corrupted?'

'Don't be revolting.'

'But that's what you want?'

Bartholomew grunted something like an affirmative. Freya had finished with the cold instrument, and now she was using something with soft hairs to brush just below my eyelid. 'You're taking this very seriously,' she said.

'I am, aren't I?' Bartholomew's tone changed as he addressed me. 'You're sure you want to do this, Lazarus? If you've got a moral objection, now's the time to tell me.'

'I'm sure, sir.'

'Not everyone's cut out for undercover work.'

'So they told me. You don't have to worry sir – the vets all tried to talk me out of it. But I want to do this.'

'Do you?' His question hung in the air. I figured I'd already answered it well enough, so I kept quiet. I could tell there was something more to come.

'This girl...' Bartholomew was treading carefully. His voice sounded like a man picking his way through cowshit. 'You're sure about the quality of her bruise?'

'Positive.'

'I see.' I heard him walking towards me, perhaps inspecting Freya's work. 'If you're right, she's the best lead we've had in years, Lazarus. We know there's some kind of... *organisation* behind the bruisers. Someone bringing in their contraband. *Procuring*. And it's starting to affect the District.'

'You really think it's that bad, sir?'

'People are even talking about changing the law. They say we can't stop all this, so we might as well legalise it. Not many, of course, but enough.' There was a disgusted snort. 'I need a win, Lazarus. To shut them up. I need something big. If this girl can lead you to the person behind the organisation...'

'...He needs to hold up his badge and say, "You're nicked, Mr Big!" Thank you, fearless leader.' I opened my eyes to watch Freya shooing Bartholomew out of the room, clearly sick of his interruptions. I looked into the mirror to see how the bruise was coming along. My eyelid was a livid purple. It was so strange to see any change at all on my face, and as Bartholomew and Freya squabbled outside, I leaned closer to the mirror and examined the bruise closely. Turned my head from side to side. Up and down. Tried to get used to it.

I don't know how long it was before I put my thumb directly over the bruise on my eyelid and began to press. I felt nothing at all as my eyeball gradually squashed out of shape under the pressure, just the sensation of matter being displaced. I pressed harder and harder, wondering if I might awaken something deep inside, hit a nerve that had been disconnected for centuries. I wondered if the City would allow me to push my eye all the way into my brain and still not allow me to feel a single twinge of pain.

And then Freya bustled back and I whipped my hand away before she could see.

I was like a little boy.

Maybe that's one of the reasons she noticed me, because I was so terrible. Maybe she took pity on someone so clearly out of their depth. I don't know. But I look back on how I contrived to 'meet' her and I laugh.

For starters, I was wearing sunglasses indoors. It wasn't even bright outside, and if I was any kind of decent undercover agent I would have waited for a different day so that my cover made a bit more sense. Instead, I'd followed her into a magic store and was trying to figure out how to 'accidentally' run into her. The trouble was I had no idea about magic and found myself skulking around the store trying to think of a good opening line. I'd rehearsed a couple of ideas on the way, but each time I approached her they suddenly seemed absurdly artificial. The brief was to strike up a conversation and then to lower my sunglasses just far enough for her to see Freya's black eye. If she really was a bruiser we were sure this would be like a secret handshake. We'd become instant friends and she'd hopefully introduce me to her suppliers. The trouble was I just couldn't think of anything to say, let alone a way to lower my sunglasses without it looking contrived. Desperate for inspiration, I began to sweat. I headed for the opposite end of the store so I wouldn't meet her unprepared and began to look around for a conversation starter. She was browsing through the illusions, chatting casually to the store-keeper, and I was reduced to looking at crystal balls with pictures of monkeys on them. I'd never seen magic in my Old Life, and although I'd seen performances since my resurrection, generating the enthusiasm I'd need to establish common ground was proving a challenge.

I gave up on the usual tricks and began to browse in the section full of ventriloquist gear and decorative dolls. I was surprised by the level of detail – some of them were almost lifelike. I picked one up and cradled it, examining its face. The skin was soft; not realistic exactly, but slightly unnerving nonetheless. It was like holding a tiny person.

I suddenly became aware of somebody standing next to me. I looked up and it was her.

I don't think she suspected anything. On the contrary, she didn't even acknowledge me as she looked up at the dolls. I'd never seen her seen this closely before, and suddenly all the undercover stuff was swept away as I realised just how gorgeous she was. Short black hair framed a heart-shaped face. She had a small, mischievous mouth, made for whispering dirty jokes, and a tiny upturned nose. It was her eyes that got me though: they were a smoky green, and there was something sad about them even when she smiled.

She took down a doll and turned to look at me. 'Do you think this looks like me?'

Sweat trickled down my forehead.

'Um...'

'I know the hair's not very similar, but that's easily fixed. It's the face I'm really interested in. What do you think?'

She held the doll next to her face to allow me to make a comparison. The resemblance was actually pretty close. I nodded and then wiped my brow. I was trying to think of a casual way to lower my sunglasses, but I felt too self-conscious. This girl was smart. She'd see straight through me.

'You think so? OK...' She looked at the remaining dolls a final time to make sure she hadn't missed a better option. Satisfied, she glanced at me to say thank you.

My glasses slipped down my sweaty nose. Not far, but enough for her to see the bruise.

It was like putting blood in the water.

She reached out and gently pushed my sunglasses back up my nose. She looked over at the door, then back to me and for the first time I saw the panther-hunger in her eyes. I knew what she wanted, and I immediately walked out of the store. There was a brief wait while she paid for her doll, and then she exited the magic shop. Without looking at me, she walked off down the street and I followed.

I wasn't quite sure what should happen next. It was a powerful feeling to have such a gorgeous girl suddenly turn that hungry look in your direction, but I didn't know how far my role as an undercover agent allowed me to go. What did Bartholomew think would happen once I made contact with this girl? Maybe he'd just assumed I'd be too disgusted to ever have sex with a bruiser, but it was obvious that *something* was about to happen, and if it was consensual I was fairly sure it wasn't against the law.

But even if it wasn't... should I go through with it? Had I misled her? I tried to wave the complicated feelings away, but at that moment, walking along with my hidden bruise and my secret girlfriend, I felt deliciously dangerous. I was *different* to the people I passed on the street. I was doing something wrong, something *sick*, and it was precisely this sickness that had attracted this girl to me.

One block away from her apartment, I took off my sunglasses.

I was too shy to leave them off for long, and virtually all of the Citizens I passed didn't even notice, but just as I was about to turn into the doorway of her building I caught the eye of a small boy. Like all children he lacked the ability to filter his reactions, and a mixture of wonder and bafflement moved across his face as he stared at my black eye. Part of me felt ashamed to have exposed myself to him in this way, but part of me also felt exhilarated. I didn't react, didn't want to cause a scene; I just kept walking through the door and up the stairs. Halfway up I began to run until I saw her face looking down at me. One more round of stairs and then we were both inside her apartment with the door safely closed against the District outside.

I put my sunglasses on the table and she smiled at me with that mischievous mouth. 'You took a risk,' she said. 'First time?'

I shrugged a little shrug. Nervous. Naked without the sunglasses.

She put the doll down on the table. 'You ever used one of these before?'

I looked into her sad green eyes. If I lied to her she'd know. 'You know I haven't.' I touched my bruise. 'I've never done anything like this before. I just...'

'Really? Never?' She quickly walked across the kitchen, reaching out to examine my black eye. She didn't ask my permission, but I knew I couldn't stop her. Her fingers were pale, delicate. She traced Freya's handiwork lightly and I could feel the pressure of her touch through the latex without any of the specifics. It was an oddly disconnected feeling, like a tiny sliver of my face had gone numb. I wanted to know if her hands were hot or cold, wanted to feel her fingerprints on my face. I wanted to know how she *felt*.

She took her hand away and looked at me searchingly. 'It's good,' she said. 'Very good. Why'd you show it to me?'

I almost said something about her bruise, but stopped myself just in time. As far as she knew, we'd only met today. 'I didn't. My glasses slipped and you saw. After that, I was following your lead.'

'Is that what happened?'

'That's the story I'm sticking to.'

'I see.' She patted my cheek before walking back to the table, and then began to carefully position the doll, moving its limbs away from its body so that it lay spread-eagled like a skydiver. Then she picked up a large kitchen knife, weighing it in her hand. Almost absent-mindedly, she pressed the edge of the knife against her wrist, rocking the blade back and forth. I watched her skin give under the pressure, but it didn't break or bleed. It simply *stopped*. She persisted for a second and then lifted the blade away.

'It probably doesn't matter about the hair,' she said. 'Normally I'd fix it, but if this is your first time, we should just get started.'

I didn't know what she was about to do. I'd never seen anything like this before.

She stared down at the doll that looked like her, and then stabbed it in the face.

Did it again.

And again.

Not frenzied or hysterical, but still tearing the face apart.

She handed me the knife and I hesitated for a second. This felt wrong, but wrong in an *exciting* way, the same way I felt when people saw my black eye. Bartholomew. The kid.

She picked up the doll and held it against her chest. Nodded for me to attack. For some reason, that's what did it. I stabbed and slashed. I felt the knife pass through the doll, through her blouse, and slam into her skin. I tore at the doll that looked like her until it fell completely to pieces, and then I stood, breathing heavily as she looked down at the mess I'd made of her blouse.

Then she smiled that mischievous smile at me, grabbed me by the collar and started licking the bruise off my face.

Her name was Rosa and she was naked. I was carefully caressing the underside of her left breast. A blackberry-purple stain was slowly spreading beneath my fingers, and just looking at it made me feel twinges of sympathetic discomfort. It wasn't genuine – that was impossible – but the illusion triggered a *memory* of pain, and that in turn stimulated a kind of psychological response. The resulting sensation was the closest I could get to real pain within the City of the Saved.

The rest of Rosa's body was similarly black and blue, as if she'd been beaten systematically with an iron bar. Her eyes were closed and she looked utterly relaxed. More than that – she looked magnificent. With a little make-up and lighting, we'd created a work of art on her body. Once upon a time I'd have been disgusted. Once upon a time I'd have reported the both of us. But now...

I'd never harmed anyone in my life. I just wasn't that kind of man. Of course there had been violence since I became a police officer, but even then the City had made sure that I never actually *hurt* anyone. That's why I'd come here. Outside of Drausinus District, the only thing people wanted to ask about was death, but here, talk like that was banned. I liked that. I liked what the District stood for, liked the positivity of their stance on celebrating life and living it to the fullest. Frankly, I couldn't understand why anyone in the City wouldn't feel the same way. We walked around in literal miracles – bodies that would never sicken, never die and never feel pain. When so many people would have killed for such a gift, it felt churlish at best to complain about those bodies, to deface them. At worst, it felt revolting, a self-absorbed kick in the face for those less fortunate than we. But now, watching bruises slowly forming under my hands, I felt slightly giddy with a kind of power. There were so many magical things in the City, but this ability to mark somebody with the gentlest caress was the most intoxicating thing I'd ever experienced. It made me feel special, like I knew *secrets*.

Finally I straightened up and washed the make-up off my hands. I flipped down a mirror and Rosa sat up and opened her eyes. We'd covered her entire body, and I saw the look of surprise on her face at the lividity of the contusions. Then I saw the phantom pain crash through her. For just a moment, I could tell she *felt* the bruising, and she staggered a little under the psychological onslaught. She started to cry and I stood paralysed, unsure what to do next. Rosa turned to look at me. I could tell that her tears were a mix of pain and joy, a weird emotional cocktail that she couldn't have achieved in any other way. I carefully reached out and dabbed at her tears. She took my hand in hers and kissed my fingers soundly. I saw a ghost of that mischievous smile. 'Your turn.'

The cop part of me froze, weighing the advantages of whether to go through with this.

The rest of me didn't hesitate. 'Do whatever you want,' I said.

It took her four hours.

She blindfolded me for the entire process, and in all that time, I never stopped debating what I should do next. With all her make-up and equipment, Rosa almost certainly had links to professional bruisers, and if I could get information out of her, I'd be on my way to Mr Big. But it was more than that, though. I just had so many questions to ask, and I'd never met someone like her before. Not in my first life, and not in this.

'Why are you here?' I said. It wasn't the question I meant to ask.

'The rent's handsome and the men are cheap.'

'No... I mean in the District.'

'Lucky. I thought you were going to get philosophical there for a minute.' I felt her tying something around my knee, cinching it tight. 'Ever hear the one about the masochist living with the sadist? The masochist keeps saying 'hurt me!' and the sadist keeps saying 'no.''

It took me a second, but I laughed.

'Ever since I got here, that's me all the time,' she said. I heard her moving something heavy into position, but I couldn't imagine what it might be. 'In my old life, people made a lot of assumptions about me. They thought I was sick. Mentally ill. I'm definitely *different*; that's a fair description. But here's the thing you need to know about me: I'm *proud* of that difference. I'm proud of the fact that the thing I need is hard to get. And I'm proud of how strong I need to be in order to get it.'

She was rubbing something on my leg now. It was probably make-up, but it was hard to tell. The tourniquet had made the whole thing numb. 'Is that what you call yourself?' I asked. 'A masochist?' We hadn't had words like that in my day; it sounded strange to me.

'I'm...' she stopped herself and there was a long pause. 'The first time I really figured it out... I'd just had my ears pierced. Some people get it done really young, but my father wouldn't let me until I turned sixteen. They told me it wouldn't hurt. They were lying. It did hurt. Not a lot, but enough. This tiny little sting and then this hot feeling. It was all over so quickly, but I just sat there feeling so embarrassed by how... good I felt. How horny.' She stopped again, and I could tell she was smiling. 'They told me I was brave. That was... weird, but I played along like a normal person and tried to sit still in the car on the way home. I told my dad I felt sick when I got home, but really it was just an excuse to get to bed. To be alone with myself.'

'You were sixteen?'

'Sweet sixteen and never been cut.' She'd finished with my leg and now she was doing something to my chest. More make-up by the feel of it. 'I can't explain it to you if it isn't your thing. It's like trying to explain an orgasm to a virgin. It's not that I don't like ordinary vanilla sex. I do – the same way I like ordinary vanilla ice-cream. But if I want to come really, *really* hard, I need the pain. That's just the way I'm wired up.'

She stopped again. 'And then there was the day that I died. It was a little bit like having my ears pierced. A sting and then warmth and then...' Her voice drained of colour. 'And then here. Where everything's perfect. I couldn't hurt myself. Couldn't die. It was like losing one of my senses. Everybody else seemed so pleased, but I just felt *crippled*. Like what I wanted just wasn't important or valuable or *allowed*.'

Something wet was trickling down my chest. I flinched a little at the cold. 'And I know this sounds crazy, but when I heard about this District I couldn't wait to get here. It should be the worst place, the very *worst* place for someone like me to live. I know their laws are stupid. But that's the thing: if I can't do the things I used to, at least I can define myself against my opposites. Feel strong again. And you want to know the crazy thing? Doing all this bruiser stuff in the one place it's not allowed... that makes it *better*. Gives it a kick. Helps me feel a tiny bit like me again.'

Rosa took the blindfold off. 'So,' she said. 'That's why I'm here.'

She took a step back and flipped the mirror down.

She'd cut my leg off. I literally couldn't see it anymore – there was just a bloody stump. What's more she'd found the scars on my chest and opened them up. Blood was everywhere and the sight of it was like a punch in the stomach. I was mutilated. I don't know exactly how she'd done it – it must be lighting, make-up and mirrors, and I didn't dare move lest I break the illusion – but she'd torn me apart. The memory of agony cascaded through me, and after nearly three centuries of being locked inside a suit of unbreakable flesh, it felt incredible. I began psychologically spiralling, falling away from myself, and it was only when Rosa touched my face with her cold hands that I realised that it felt like I'd been dying.

The cop part of me didn't miss the opportunity. I looked straight at her and said, 'Where can we go *further*?'

The guy sitting closest to us was slumped forward, his eyes unseeing. Judging by the number of kool-aid bottles in front of him, he was as dead as it was possible to get. I'd seen the stuff before – even drunk it a couple of times in the Districts where it was legal – and I knew how powerful it could be. Bruisers liked it because it slowed down the brain functions. It meant you could achieve the nearest thing to death without triggering the City's safety protocols. It wasn't very dignified, and the nausea that kicked in the morning after was awful, but then the bruisers were probably quite happy with that little side-effect. It wasn't pain, but beggars can't be choosers.

Rosa put her arms around me and smiled. I could tell she was waiting for something to happen. I wasn't allowed to drink any kool-aid – the speakeasy had some kind of entrance requirement before that was allowed – and she was abstaining out of solidarity. I'd noticed a few other non-drinkers dotted throughout the crowd. Presumably they were new as well.

I pushed aside Rosa's headscarf to expose the bruise behind her ear, and then leaned in to kiss it gently. I felt her stiffen at my touch, and she quickly took the scarf off to allow me unimpeded access. Normally I might have felt inhibited, but in a place as dimly lit as this, and surrounded by people who might as well be dead, it hardly seemed to matter.

Suddenly a spotlight raked the audience. We froze, watching the light as it picked over the dead members of the audience and stopped on those that clearly hadn't drunk the kool-aid. There was the sound of footsteps from the stage as the spot slowly made its way toward us, and when it finally halted on my face, a voice rang out. 'Come on up, soldier. You need to tell us a story.'

I looked at Rosa. 'What kind of story?' I whispered.

She smiled at me. 'Everybody new has to tell a story about why they've come here. That's the rule.' She kissed my fingers and I stood up. The spotlight followed me all the way to the stage. I slowly made my way up the stairs, my brain working overtime. I'd constructed an entire backstory for occasions like this, but a part of me, the part that had spoken to undercover veterans, was inclined to simply be as truthful as possible. Simply put, the truth was easier to remember. That's why I was Lazarus to Rosa and that's why, for the most part, I'd tried to dodge the truth about myself rather than lie to her outright. As I walked across to the host and his microphone, I decided telling the truth was the best option, but the idea of doing so was completely terrifying.

'What's your name, soldier?' said the host.

'Lazarus.'

'No relation to *that* Lazarus, are you?' Everybody out in the dark laughed, and the host grinned at me.

'Actually, a pretty close relation.' More laughter. I looked into the audience and saw Rosa's face. She was smiling at me, but I could tell she was also a little intrigued.

'Seriously? What was he, your uncle, your dad, your...'

'Closer than that. *I'm* Lazarus.'

There was a ripple of nerves through the dark. I heard someone walking out and a door banging behind them. I took the microphone from the host. I didn't look down at Rosa again, didn't want to know her reaction. I just started talking.

'You've probably heard some things about me. A lot of people have. When I arrived in the City, I wasn't ready for that. They knew my name and where I'm from and all kinds of stuff. But the one thing they thought they knew about me – the really important thing – well, they were wrong about that.

'"Lazarus, come forth!" Everyone in the City had heard those words. Everyone except me. I knew the man who *said* those words. He was a friend of mine. I don't like to talk about him for the same reason I don't like to talk about me. For a start, people don't believe you when you tell them the truth, but also because...' I paused a moment to consider how to phrase this. 'Because he's the reason I'm here in Drausinus District.

'The last thing I remember is being thirsty. Being sick and thirsty and my sister's face telling me she'd sent for my friend Yeshua. I remember being pleased to hear his name. I'd heard about the things he'd been doing. The miracles. The politics. But I didn't get involved in all that. I was just his friend who'd cooked for him, made all the loaves and fishes myself, told him jokes. He was a big laugher. That's something no one remembers about him.

'And then I was born again, just like you. But for some reason everybody thought I had prior experience. And that's when things started getting strange.' I began to pick my words carefully now as I sailed closer to the present day. 'People started coming to me. People of faith. I discovered that somehow there were stories about me in their holy books, "Lazarus come forth" and so on, and that made me special. They wanted to talk to me about what they should do now they were resurrected. I tried to tell them I had no idea what they were talking about. Yeshua was my friend – that was it. He hadn't done any miracles on me. I had just as much experience of resurrection as they did. But they didn't believe me. They wanted to hear what they wanted to hear. They didn't want to know about my life. The only thing that was special about me, apparently, was that I'd died and then come back. That's all they wanted me to be.'

I looked out at Rosa again. 'And that's not who I was. So I tried to disappear. But they found me again and again and again, until finally, I heard about this place. Drausinus District. The one place in the City where it's illegal to talk about death or injury or any of that fun stuff. The one place I thought I'd get some peace.'

'But why are you *here*?' said the host.

I was about to say something when the lights went out. Strong hands grabbed my arms and dragged me off the stage. Then something smashed into the back of my head and everything slipped away.

'I know you're a cop.'

I was sitting down, tied up and blindfolded again. The voice was male, and it sounded tired and careworn. There was something familiar about it that was nagging at me, but I couldn't put my finger on why.

'I'm not a cop.'

'Please.'

'My name's Lazarus...'

'I know that as well.' There was a hint of impatience in the voice now. 'Your name's Lazarus and you're an undercover cop. You're looking for the Mr Big of the bruiser network. Your girlfriend's name is Rosa, and she likes to pretend to kill herself. She's pretty good at it. In fact, as far as I know, she's the best there is.'

'I'll tell her you're a fan.'

'She's the best. Trust me.'

'Trust you? I don't even know you.'

'Oh, that's not true.'

'Is there a reason I'm here?'

I heard footsteps coming towards me and then the blindfold was torn away. I blinked in the light, trying to make sense of the face in front of me.

It was mine.

'I want you to kill me,' said my face.

Suddenly a lot of things began to fall into place. I stared at him, trying to take in what this meant. He was older than me by at least fifteen years, but essentially he was still the same man. There were no scars or moles or anything to distinguish us. We were the same man. But if that was true, then that would mean...

'*You're* the one ,' I said. '"Lazarus come forth." That's you.'

'I see my reputation precedes me.'

'So you *were* resurrected?'

'The City seems to think so. Why else would there be two of us?'

'So why do you want him to kill you?' said Rosa's voice.

I turned my head to see her tied up in a corner. She looked just as surprised as me, but I could hear the anger in her voice. From that point, I knew that whatever happened next it was over between us.

My older self – let's just call him Mr Big – walked over to his desk and leaned against it. 'I want him to kill me because I can't die,' he said.

'Why me though? What can I do?'

He stared at me levelly. 'When he brought me back... Yeshua did a clean job.' he began. 'At least I think he did. When I walked out of that tomb it felt like being born. But the City...' He looked at me carefully, watching for my reaction. 'When it brought you back... do you feel like there's something *missing*?'

'You heard what I said on stage. I'm guessing that's why I'm here.'

'And I know a little bit how you feel. I went through the same kind of thing when Yeshua brought me back. The funny thing was, after that first resurrection life felt *valuable* to me. Like I had so much to *do*.'

'But now?'

'Now... there's something missing.' He picked up a tiny razor blade from his desk and placed it in the corner of his mouth. 'You know there are legends about us – about me – that aren't true. They say I didn't smile at all after I got resurrected that first time. That one's bullshit.' He pushed the blade hard into his mouth, tugging it up into a grotesque half-smile. Once upon a time he would have sliced his face apart, but now his mouth just stretched until it would stretch no more. I saw his knuckles whitening as he tried to push the 'smile' wider, but the blade slipped out. He tossed it aside. 'Second time around though,' he said, his voice still calm and tired. 'It's absolutely true. Something about this place, this body... it's like everything's numb.'

'You don't have to live here,' said Rosa. 'You could go outside the City. Do whatever you like.'

'True. But the thing is, what if the next time I get resurrected... what if it gets worse? What if lose something *more*?' He stared at both of us with eyes like ash. 'I've done it all, Laz. Tried to find a point. But if there's no pain, *real* pain you've got nothing to measure the good stuff against. Without an end point, life's just not *urgent*. I want to feel *everything* and fuck knows I've tried, but this City's always there to keep things nice and *safe*.' He spat the last word out, the first real emotion he'd exhibited.

'So that's why you're... Mr Big?'

He shrugged. 'You look for the loopholes in the protocols long enough, sooner or later you figure out a way to monetise them. It's not like the money's helped me get what I really want. The City doesn't take bribes.'

'But you think I do?'

'You're a cop, Laz. Of course you don't take bribes.'

I looked at Rosa quickly, and then back at him. 'Oh, that's not true.'

'The cop part or the bribe part?'

'The bribe part. I think I know why you need the cop part.'

'Do you? I can see why you became a police officer.'

Rosa's eyes narrowed. 'Am I missing something?'

'He wants me to kill him...'

'...Yeah, but he can't die. Not in the City.'

'No. We can't murder his body, but we might be able to murder his *life*. And if he were to commit *suicide*...' Rosa's eyes widened. I could see her mind racing at furious speed. I turned back to Mr Big. 'You're going to have to tell me everything if you want me to do this.'

'Is this the cop part or the bribe part talking?'

'What do you care as long as I kill you?'

It didn't take Rosa long to figure out what to do. She made some phone calls, rummaged around in her apartment and finally laid out her plan in detail. I didn't like it very much, but I thought it would work. Certainly I couldn't think of a better way to achieve the same psychological effect, and so I made my own phone calls and then we arranged to meet Mr Big at the speakeasy.

When we got there he'd closed it for the night. We sat at the bar and he served us drinks and cigarettes. I thought he might ask us questions about what was going to happen next, but he barely said a word. Rosa chatted away to me, but he simply concentrated on keeping our glasses topped up.

Finally, I checked my watch. 'What are you going to call yourself when this is all over?' I asked.

'I really hadn't thought about it,' he said. 'Mr Small, maybe? I'm sure something will come to me.'

Rosa smiled. She looked down at her bag of tricks sitting next to the bar. She was just about to speak when something heavy smashed into the speakeasy's front door. All of us jumped and spun around. There was another mighty smash.

I looked at my counterpart. 'Do you think it's a raid?'

His face twisted. 'You tell me.'

Rosa had ducked down next to the bar. She unzipped her bag and pulled out a jerrycan. She unscrewed the top, placed it on the ground and then kicked it over. The smell of petrol immediately filled the room. Just as Mr Big was yelling at her, just as Bartholomew's boys broke through the outside door, she flicked a match.

The hungry bellow of the flames deafened us all. Rosa climbed on the bar, grabbed bottles of alcohol from the wall behind her and threw them to all four points of the speakeasy. Mr Big was simply dumbfounded at her actions, and the vice squad were equally surprised when they were met by a hail of bottles as they stormed through the shattered doorway. The flames caught the alcohol and forced the officers back – surprising rather than hurting them of course, but buying us time. I grabbed Rosa's bag, joined her on the bar and hauled the dumbfounded Mr Big up alongside us. Through the smoke I could just make out Bartholomew beating the fire out on his uniform, and I knew we had to get out of sight as quickly as possible.

We charged along the bar, leapt over the flames and ran for the interior door. Mr Big shouldered through it and kept running. I chased after him while Rosa stopped to lock the door behind us. Mr Big knew the place better than I did, but my policeman's fitness gave me the edge. After a minute's pursuit, I smacked him in the back of the head and sent him careering into the wall of the corridor. He snarled at me and fought back, raining blows upon my face, biting and clawing at me as I used my weight to slowly bring him to the ground. In the City, this was all you needed to do to arrest anybody. You could cause and receive no pain, you simply had to wait for your colleagues to arrive in order to completely subdue a criminal. Mr Big knew that as well as I did, and as I gradually brought him to his knees, he snapped at my face, my eyes, anything he could think of in order to break my hold. But it was no good. I felt his knees buckle and I kicked out at precisely the right moment, taking his legs from under him. We fell to the floor, still struggling painlessly and silently. 'Come on, ' I whispered. 'The first thing you knew about me was that I was a cop.'

He screamed in frustration, wriggling and cursing. He was so loud he didn't hear Rosa walking up behind us. Didn't hear her unzip her bag and pull out the second jerrycan.

The petrol soaked us in a matter of seconds. Rosa stood back and lit another match. I saw the look on her face, the tiny fire dancing in her eyes. At the moment she threw the match I looked down at Mr Big; saw anger and confusion chasing across his face.

Then the fire ate us up.

There was no pain, but there was *power*; a roaring, consuming fist that grasped our bodies and literally took our breath away. I felt my eyelashes burning, my tongue drying out in milliseconds, and my nose filled with the smell of my blazing clothes. Everything on the surface of our bodies was being devoured and I held my counterpart tight, refusing to allow him to roll and put out the flames. I held him the way I'd held Rosa the very first time.

Finally the flames began to run out of combustible fuel and I relaxed my grip a little. The look on my double's face was one of total shock, and I gently stroked his scalp, extinguishing the last guttering flames. The final remnants of his hair fell away beneath my fingers, revealing the smooth, undamaged skin beneath. I licked his blackened face, my tongue rasping on the ash. More shiny, light-brown skin appeared. He stared at me as I did this and I kissed his eyes in order to close them. Then I whispered in his ear, 'Lazarus, go forth.'

I stood then, naked and blackened, shaking my body like a dog to extinguish the last of the flames. The walls were alight, but not enough to harm this part of the building. I'd need to fix that. In the distance I could hear Bartholomew and his boys smashing through the interior door, and I hoisted Mr Big onto his feet and gave Rosa the nod. She handed me the last jerrycan.

My double didn't physically need Rosa to support him, but psychologically he was smashed. I leaned in and kissed Rosa, the soot from my lips leaving a final bruise behind, and then I spoke my last words to the man that had been Lazarus. 'Get out. I'm going undercover so you can be dead.'

I saw the realisation behind his eyes, and then I was emptying petrol over everything as Rosa dragged him away. The last thing he would have seen was me walking off into the flames of his old life, towards the police officers.

I hope that killed him.

I hope.

My name used to be Lazarus.

Once upon a time I was the Mr Big of the bruiser network in Drausinus District. I ran the speakeasies, shipped the kool-aid, the make-up and all the other fun stuff. I did that for a very long time.

And then I killed myself and burned down my entire life for good measure. The whole network, everyone I knew... I betrayed them all. I just walked out of the fire and told the police everything they wanted to know. A lot of people got away – someone seems to have tipped them off before the raids really started – but everything I built is ashes now.

My name used to be Lazarus, but that name's dead now. That life.

The girl got me out. Washed me. Told me to get out of the District before the police did their big round-up. I didn't hear all of what she said because I just kept watching my skin as the soot was wiped away. There was no hair anywhere. No dirt. Everything was clean. I don't know why exactly, but as I looked in the mirror at the bald man staring back, I began to cry.

The girl wouldn't come with me. She walked me to the edge of the District and then told me I could go where I liked. I asked her why she wouldn't come with me and she said nothing had changed for her. The only difference now was that there was a vacancy for a Mr Big in the District. The one person who couldn't fill that vacancy was me, she said. After all, she'd killed me herself. She was very proud of that.

I gave in, turned and crossed the border. The strangest thing was that I was already starting to think of myself as a different person. My responsibilities, my past, all of it had been burned. I had no choice but to think fresh thoughts now, and that meant the first shoots of my new personality were peeking through. The one thing that nagged me was what had driven my other self to give me this gift? Why had he done this for me and why had he taken the fall in order to make it work? Unless, perhaps it wasn't just me that had died in that fire? Perhaps, in assuming my identity so completely, Lazarus the cop had seen a way to kill himself as well...?

I don't know. I probably never will. What I do know is that I need a new name. It used to be Lazarus, but that name is taken now. I can't go back. I'll have to think about a fresh one very carefully. What we call ourselves is important, particularly when you're starting a new life. I've got no idea what I'm eventually going to call myself, and even less about the kind of man I'm going to be.

But sooner or later I'll be someone.

APOCALYPSE DAY

Philip Purser-Hallard

The City, like all cities, is a living thing: always in flux, growing and breathing, a process as much as a place. A thriving business district, all skyscrapers and aircars, can become derelict at the whim of some microscopic eddy in the ebb and flow of the City's local gigaeconomics, creating skeletal homes for australopithecine tribes and nomadic aerial Citizens. Later those ruins might themselves become a tourist attraction, bringing in jobs and income and eventual gentrification, with refurbished monoliths now housing upwardly-mobile City-born Hive collectives.

Across Yerba Buena Bay, Motet Hill has also changed. Over the centuries of City living, the decorative suburb has been at different times a fishing community, an airship port with housing for its aircrews and stevedores, and a popular site for holiday homes, handy for the bay and for the ruins. During the past few decades, it has been transforming itself into a respectable leisure and retail zone for the surrounding suburbs, and by some fluke of urban lack-of-planning Armistice Street has become its main drag, with shops and bars and boutiques stretching nearly to the hilltop.

At Number 67 stands The World Turned Upside Down, a bar known informally to locals as the World. Its frontage is a low, glass-fronted, concrete-roofed extension to what was once a pretty shingled townhouse. It affects a faux-antique pub-sign: one side shows an inverted snowglobe containing the City; the other an upturned church and graveyard, from which the dead of all human species are being shaken into the sky beneath.

Despite this touch of last-universe pretension, the tavern's interior is functional and even spartan, with wooden benches around the walls, and hard stools at the granite-topped bar. A handful of patrons are scattered around its interior: a slender-limbed, heavy-browed Citizen of Neanderthal and Lunarian stock; a trio of Parthian archers on their way to the front lines; an apparently human-normal man dressed in a tasteful kilt and cloth-of-gold poncho.

At the bar sit two men: one tallish, his good looks betraying a caution borne of experience regarding the likely behaviour of the world at large; the other older-looking, rumpled, his clothes defiantly unfashionable. A sticking-plaster on his neck shows that he has cut himself shaving, which is a chilling sign of the times.

Behind the bar, a cyclops is washing glasses, holding each up to his eye to check for smears before returning it to the shelf. At seven feet he is nearly as tall as his hybrid customer, and gangles like an adolescent boy.

The inn's amenities include a media holoscape set into one corner of the ceiling. It is turned to News 2.4 X 10^6, one of the KaneNet news channels, and is gradually infusing everybody in the World with a sense of burgeoning unease.

...throughout a fifty-megameter-square area of the Western Quarter, previously unaffected by the Civil War, the anchorhuman is saying. *All contact has been lost with the affected area, centred on Bonehall District. Eye-witness reports are confused at present, but it appears the effect may be spreading. We'll have the latest on the phenomenon as it develops...*

The City is a living thing. And like all living things, it can die.

Calafia District, like Bonehall, has been largely unscathed by the fading of the City's invulnerability protocols and the consequent, inevitable Civil War. Not so in all Districts, as some of the human flotsam washed up by its waves in Yerba Buena can attest.

'They took her,' the younger-looking man at the bar is saying. He wears a long overcoat over a v-neck sweater, shirt and tie. 'Soon as the Civil War started, before we'd heard anything of it out in Cerulean, they found us and they took her. I was away from our platform, taking some tourists out on a flight, and those bastards came in wearing daedalopters and snatched her right away. I never did find out whether it was Greeks or Trojans got her.'

'Bastards,' echoes the other man, into his alcohol-free lager. 'You're sure it was one or the other, then?'

'Well, I –' the first man stops short. 'Damn, Faber, I never thought of that. I guess... with Helénē's reputation, it could have been all kinds of people. We'd never troubled much with making ourselves hard to find.'

'It must be difficult,' the rumpled man, Faber, observes after a pause. 'Not knowing where she is or what's happened to her. Worse I expect than...' he trails off.

The first man glances at him. 'Yeah, I heard about your friend.'

Faber shrugs. 'He'd made a lot of enemies.' He nods at the holoscape. 'I must say this sort of thing puts it all into perspective. Did that newsreader just say "apophatic"?'

The man in the overcoat grunts. 'Search me. So what, you think this is some kind of new weapon?'

'I haven't a clue,' Faber admits. 'If it is, it's on an unprecedented scale. Within the City, at least.'

The barman has been listening quietly. He says, 'I don't understand why it's happened in Bonehall. Brianna says it's a perfectly ordinary Stone Age District, all standing stones and wooden huts, with a few hill-forts just for show. Why would anyone attack a place like that?'

'Why assume it's targeted?' Faber asks.

The cyclops considers. 'What other possibilities are there? A random act of terrorism?'

'Weapons trial gone wrong?' the tall man suggests.

Faber shrugs again. 'It always pays to consider the alternatives.'

The afternoon, and the apocalypse, wear on. At some point the Parthian squaddies leave, to kick up a riot in the louder bars closer to the waterfront.

...absorbed into an increasing volume of what archemathicists are calling 'apophatic space', the Kane News anchor is saying, visibly worried now. *At present the sphere is less*

than a gigameter in diameter, but the effect is spreading at what appears to be exponential speed...

The barman occasionally glances at his watch, blinking his great eye in consternation. 'They're late,' he says eventually, just before the door to the street bursts open to admit two newcomers.

The woman, a freckled redhead, wears jeans and a crop-top. A teenage resurrectee like the cyclops, her clothing shows off her youthful figure to its full advantage. 'Akroates!' she cries, and runs to hug the barman as he emerges to greet her. 'Inigo! Moody!' she adds, embracing the two men at the bar. 'It is such a delight to see all of you again!'

'The feeling's mutual, Miss Maitland,' the tall man, Moody, says as he submits to her embrace. 'I hardly recognised you.'

'Oh, please,' the woman says, 'you must all call me Sophy! I can only apologise for how stiffly conventional you must have found me when last we saw one another.'

'Well, we've all changed,' Faber observes.

A cough from behind Sophy recalls to her the presence of her travelling companion. 'Oh, my dear,' she says, 'I am so forgetful of my manners today!' She ushers forward a pleasant, slightly bewildered-looking man in a dark-blue tabard and jeans which match her own. 'Dear friends, allow me to present my husband, Mr Edward Davenport-Maitland. Edward, these are my deme-kin: Akroates, Terrance Moody and Inigo Faber.'

'It's great to meet you all at last,' Edward asserts hopefully, but with a nervous edge. 'Sophy has been eager for us all to get together since Highbury's been liberated.'

'After all, beloved, you have met my *other* family,' Sophy reminds him. 'This allows you to complete the set.'

'Well, not quite –' Faber begins.

Akroates has opened the interior door behind the bar, and bellows upstairs, 'Brianna! Jane! They're here!'

'How is dear Jane?' asks Sophy, lowering her voice. The family reunion has already caused the hybrid patron (who is perhaps baffled, like many City-born, at the importance of demes among the resurrectee generation) to go her way in disgust. The ponchoed man remains in the darkest corner of the bar.

'She has certain ups and downs,' Akroates tells Sophy. 'It's changed things for her. You'll see.'

'Jane's ex-boyfriend rekilled himself,' Moody explains in an undertone to Edward, seeing his befuddlement. 'Right after invulnerability ended. It was what he'd been waiting for, I guess, but Jane took it pretty hard. They say he was the first suicide in the City, but that's just because he was a musician some people'd heard of.'

Edward nods sagely. 'They say the same thing about Kurt Co–' He breaks off as the interior door opens again, and the fifth and sixth members of Sophy's deme emerge.

The blonde woman whom Sophy greets as Brianna is lissom yet sturdy, in a way which speaks of frequent exercise or ancestral gene-tweaking. The figure who follows her through the door has the body of a young girl, perhaps five years old, curled inside a nest of flexible metallic plastic equipped with strong manipulating tentacles. Without moving a muscle she leaps deftly onto the bar, and turns her expressionless face on Sophy. 'Long time no see, deme-sis,' she says flatly, her voice augmented and deepened by the cybernetic rig.

'My, Jane,' Sophy replies imperturbably. 'How you have grown.'

'Still no interest in the booze, Inigo?' Jane asks Faber, pouring herself a scotch.

'Serenely untempted,' Faber replies.

The family reunion has broken into separate conversations, observed impassively by the man in the poncho.

'What about the hemlock?' she asks maliciously.

He winces, but changes the subject. 'Have you been watching this?'

He nods at the holoscape, where a many-eyed man is telling an interviewer: *...every reason to suppose that this is a temporary localised phenomenon. Certainly these predictions of*

City-wide disaster are irresponsible scaremongering. We're sure it can't have the energy to sustain this kind of...

The spider-frame shrugs, an expressive undulating wave. 'Everything's a catastrophe these days.' Jane's voice is mechanical. 'This is just more of the same.'

'So why does she need those things?' Edward is asking Brianna.

'She doesn't,' Brianna says. 'Not physically, not since she started ageing again. But she says that being posthuman isn't something you go back on.'

'And you're her carer?' Edward asks.

Brianna looks at him in puzzlement. 'I guess,' she says. 'She needs a lot of care sometimes. Keeping her away from anything she might hurt herself with, that sort of thing. She'd order potent weapons on the omniweb if I let her. But there are compensations.'

Edward frowns. 'You mean you're... together?'

'We spend a lot of time "together", yeah.' The blonde woman smiles. 'After all, I've known her practically since she was born.'

'But where is our deme-brother Lazarus?' Sophy is asking Moody and Akroates. 'Was he detained by his work?'

A glance passes between Moody and the giant's single eye. 'We've had no reply to his invitation,' Akroates admits. 'I contacted his employers in Drausinus, and they said he doesn't work there any more. They seemed quite peeved about it, actually.'

'Nobody's heard from Laz in years,' says Moody. 'Since before the Civil War. We think maybe he got sick of people bothering him and went into hiding. Like Jane's brother keeps doing.'

'Still,' Akroates points out, 'the invitation was keyed to his biodata. It should have found him wherever he was.'

'Oh, but what a shame,' says Sophy. 'I looked forward so to the seven of us being together again.'

'Excuse me a moment.' Akroates crosses to his one remaining customer as he sits quietly in the corner. 'Can I get you another drink, my friend?'

The man shakes his head. 'I'm good,' he says.

'Have you come from the front lines?' the cyclops asks, causing the man to frown.

'Why do you ask?' His voice is unnaturally deep, as if disguised.

'Your synth-flesh mask,' Akroates says. 'I have a good eye,' he adds, apologetically. 'I thought perhaps you'd been in a fire.'

The man strokes the artificial cheek whose skin overwrites his real face. 'Yes,' he says. 'Yes, I was in a fire.'

Something in the stranger's bass voice causes the barman to frown for a moment, then he holds out a huge hand. 'Akroates,' he says. 'I run the World.' It's a well-worn joke.

The other clasps his fingers, hesitates for a moment, then shakes. 'Rich,' he says firmly. 'Richard Mann.'

This doomsday has invited in a plague of catastrophes.

Surreal images succeed one another across the holoscape. The Romuline District in flames, sacked by triumphant barbarians. A statue of the goddess Civitata, speaking in the Council Chamber. A man-shaped black hole walking through instantly-consumed streets, an ambulatory vanishing point. Robed, animal-headed figures striding out of pyramids, followed by shambling, bandaged hordes. And, all the while, a graphic shows the spread across the City of that sinister cloud of unknowing.

The deme and its hangers-on watch in mingled awe and horror.

'What the hell is happening out there?' Edward wonders fearfully. 'And why isn't anyone *stopping* it?'

'Who says they're not?' asks Faber. On the holoscape, domestic appliances clamber together, forming gigantic, hideous robot shapes which march upon the invading apophasis. It makes no less sense than anything else on the news today.

Richard Mann stands among them now. 'I'm sure the City's fighting it,' he says. Tacitly, charitably perhaps, the deme-mates have accepted the stranger's presence among them. Today is no time for a human being to be alone. 'Either she'll succeed and we'll live, or she'll fail and we'll die again forever.'

'Such a short history,' says Sophy. '300 years? Why, that is less by far than Rome, or Paris, or London. Our lives here were to be eternal.' There is a note of bitterness in her voice.

'Get real,' says Jane, whose voice is bitterness itself. 'This is reality. Death is. It's always been.'

'I was married to a demigoddess,' Moody says. 'Feels like I should be calling in favours.' Outside the windows of The World Turned Upside Down, the sky over Calafia District begins to *strobe*.

'What good would it do?' Akroates asks. 'The gods know we want to live.' Jane glares at him, but says nothing. 'What they decide... it's as far beyond our reach as the sky-dome itself.'

The deme's members stand in the house of resurrection and wait as the apocalypse unfolds.

'I climbed the sky-dome once,' Brianna says. 'From the Eastern Wall. You just have to use suction crampons.'

Together they watch to see what will happen next.